The Unfinished Line

KLAIR KNOX MYSTERY
BOOK ONE

Zee David

This is a work of fiction. Similarities to real people, places, or events are entirely coincidental.

THE UNFINISHED LINE

First edition. September 24, 2022.

Copyright © 2022 Zee David.

Written by Zee David.

To you, who your fingers are, sweeping through this page.

I write because you read.

Without a reason, there is no essence.

Thank you for grabbing my work!

Enjoy

Trigger Warning

This book has strong language; please read it at your discretion.

Thank you.

Save Me

She wallowed in pain.
In self-pity, she lived her life.
With prolonged sadness in her eyes, she muttered some prayers:
"Can someone help this wretched soul of mine?"
"Can someone save me?"
Then she was gifted the fruit of oblivion.
Lost in its world, she became unchained.
"Was the gift a curse or a blessing?"
She now wallows yet in self-pity.
Wondered who she is and how her life had come to become void.
Now she stares into oblivion and prays yet again,
"Can someone help me, please?"

Chapter One

K lair
I would have loved to start with my dreams, but I have forgotten them. The theme of my mind has become an illusion, and remembering facts has become an ordeal for me.

On top of it all, I can't seem to recall the dream I had a few seconds ago. It is bothersome, as if it is scratching at the back of my head like a cat clawing its way out of an enclosed space. I can still feel it eating at me from within.

Thinking about it isn't solving anything.

I try going back to bed, envisioning myself all wrapped up in a soft woolly blanket, dreaming of nuts and caramels.

That's exactly what my therapist has suggested. I know it isn't going to work, even as I squeeze my eyes shut. I listen as the clock ticks, the seconds turning into minutes. I listen to the soft whistle of the wind as it travels over the shores. I count to six hundred, then wait again.

As expected, it isn't working.

I sit up gingerly, glancing around for nothing. This happens every morning. At least since I can remember. The house is eerie; the silence is deafening. I keep getting the feeling that something is wrong, but my therapist says it's just my imagination. I'm always imagining things, I guess.

As she speaks from the other side of the desk at our last session, I have this strange desire to yell at her. To ask how a blank mind could imagine things. She is supposed to be the expert, after all.

There is a big t-shirt carelessly thrown on the couch beside the bed. I would have told you the color, only I can't. The color doesn't register, no matter how hard I try to force it. Most times, it ends up giving me a nasty headache and a feeling of emptiness. My therapist's diagnosis is color blindness. It is my body's way of protecting me from the trauma of an accident I cannot even remember. She doesn't exactly know if it has a cure, but she is optimistic that it will be corrected soon. I wonder how soon this "soon" is.

One might think I'm addicted to my therapist, given the amount of time I spend with her every week, as well as several different bottles of drugs lying all around, labeled *Therapist's Prescription*.

I have no idea when the accident happened or how long I have been this way, but Luke says it's been some time. I guess it depends on what he calls "some time"—years, months, days, or perhaps hours?

He says I took a sleeping pill one night because I had insomnia, but I sleepwalked into the woods and fell. I hit my head from the fall and was lucky to be alive because the ravine, which he once took me to, is full of rocks. He found me there in the early hours of the morning when he checked my room and noticed I wasn't in my bed. According to the doctor, I was medically diagnosed as comatose due to the hemorrhage in my brain caused by the trauma. The doctor did not use the word lucky, but his words meant it was a miracle I survived.

Our home is situated in a gated community, Though I haven't been able to really walk around the community, I can feel that my husband isn't telling me everything about that night. Is my husband lying to me, or just keeping a secret?

My feet touch the floor, and I cringe as the cold seeps into my body. Shivering slightly, I put on the t-shirt and the flip-flops I find on the rack before paddling my way around the room. I have no idea what I want to do, so I end up just walking in circles, thinking and feeling.

The clock strikes nine a.m., its clanging chord too loud for my ears. I lie back on the bed, then take a seat. I feel the need to wait as if I'm expecting something, only I'm not.

I wait a lot these days without a clue as to what I'm waiting for. It feels like a veil has been placed over my mind, and I can't seem to get it off.

The canvas on the other side of my room catches my attention. Its splendor and grace call to me, an echo of my name resounding in my mind. I can feel it reach its hands out to me, pulling me in a warm embrace, pulling me into an unfamiliar yet safe dance.

I get up for the second time, my legs pulling me in its direction. I try to understand why I am suddenly interested in the canvas. I have no clue what to do, yet I feel strangely confident about my choice.

My hand finds a brush, its pointed tip telling me stories of its meeting with colors. Its old handle is worn by the repeated use by someone who fancied and loved painting, but I can't find any of its produced work hanging on the walls.

I think about putting the brush down and returning to bed, frustrated at how I can't see the colors. But something is holding me back, willing me to wait yet again.

The cans of paint are lined up irregularly beside the canvas as if someone had been using them for a long time but stopped abruptly. A thin layer of dust covers the lids, but that doesn't bother me as my hands pry them open.

The palette feels so natural in my hands. I smile in excitement, glad that I'm going to do something that has nothing to do with waiting or my therapist's office.

A particular can of paint catches my attention. Its dented sides feel familiar in my hand, so I decide to use it. I gently scoop some paint onto the palette and notice the uneven markings of different strokes. It looks like the palette has been hastily wiped with some kind of sponge.

The brush hits the plain canvas, stroke after stroke. At first, I don't feel a thing. It all goes back to being unfamiliar, like I'm not there, detached, staring at myself making a stroke with the painting brush.

Now, I'm in front of a half-painted canvas, holding a palette that bears all resemblance to a hidden act. I'm not there anymore but waiting in a room or something that looks like a room. Its features are unidentifiable, a picture of a row of corridors that all look identical. There is a flash... a woman... pale eyes... in a pool of liquid.

Another flash.

This time, I'm staring at the figure. It's hazy, and I can't see its face. But I'm here: where? Something is pulling me towards the first door in the corridor. I feel the unquenchable urge to know what lies behind the door. I have seen this door somewhere. I'm sure of it.

Suddenly, I'm not there anymore, but in a hallway with strange markings and symbols. I'm in the middle of the hallway, looking around for anything that could get me out of here.

The figure is back, lying in a sort of pool.

Confusion and fear set in as I try to find my way out.

The palette clatters to the floor. My cat weaves its way between my feet, and his high tail brushes my exposed skin. I collapse in a torrent of ragged breaths; I'm confused and frustrated. Just what exactly lies behind that door? Why am I seeing these images? Why do I feel I'm missing something very important?

Mr. Sim—the cat—passes by again, staring at me as if he can sense something isn't right. I have woken up to him watching me at night. An oval-shaped pendant around his neck dangles and shines, giving me a headache. I feel bad that I can't remember him, but my husband says I have always loved him.

I push myself off the floor and make my way to the room next to mine. My husband isn't in, as expected. He works in a museum as its director and has to leave early to return late.

I don't miss him when he leaves each day because the idea of me being married still feels strange. Luke says we were college sweethearts. Though I don't remember him, I like that I can depend on him.

I like the way his hair falls over his eyes, the way his eyes watch me when he thinks I'm not looking. I like the way he calls my name, another thing I can't remember ever hearing. He calls me Klair and showed me my birth certificate as proof, so I suppose Klair must be my name.

I like the name. Still, something is wrong. My husband hates it when I speak about my flashes. He hates it when I try hard to remember.

I know he told me about what happened that night, but I still feel like it was a lie, so last night, as we ate at the dining table, I told him to tell me what happened the night of the accident. His expression became unreadable for a few moments, and it frightened me. When I pointed it out, he excused it as stress and told me not to bother myself with what happened that night.

I see how he constantly tries to evade the topic each time I bring it up. There is always a stammer, a hard stare, silence, or scolding.

He loves me. He told me that himself. And what other option do I have other than to believe him?

I walk to the small kitchen, running my hands through the utensils he said I once loved using. Ever since I got here, he has been making our meals, pointing out delicacies I enjoy.

I smile every time he does that, not wanting to hurt his feelings with a confused expression. I think he's seen it, how hard I try to hide it, yet he never complains.

I grab the plate of eggs on the kitchen counter, finding the bread right beside it. This is supposed to be my favorite food. Mr. Sim hops on the counter as I sit to eat, watching and waiting. He meows, but I ignore it. He walks away to do something else. I try, you know. I try to remember how much I used to love him, but I don't remember.

The clock shows nine thirty a.m. I feel its already clanging sound over the past minutes echoing and traveling through the unoccupied three-bedroom apartment, making the space feel emptier than it is. My husband usually calls around this time to ask if I've had breakfast. Sometimes, I feel the real reason is to check whether I'm still in the house, like he is afraid I would run off somewhere. Maybe it is just my imagination. It wouldn't be the first time it has played tricks on me.

Putting the plate back on the counter, I wonder how my husband would feel if I suddenly announced that I had gotten my memory back. Would he be excited, lifting me in his arms and whirling me around like in the movie we saw together last night? Or would he get upset, asking me for the specific details I remembered, trying to save some secret? I shouldn't have this thought about the person who claims to love me, but I can't seem to help it.

I go back to the canvas. I try to decipher what could have triggered those flashes. My therapist says it occurred when I saw or heard something that had happened before. But what was it?

I try looking at it one way, tilting it the other way around, hoping it would spark something. I try going back into my head, trying to focus on images. I just want to remember something, anything. Why is it so hard? That scratching feeling is back again, this time much more violent and forceful... I push my way through it, fueled by my desire to get an answer. The only thing that returns is the hazy face of the woman lying on the floor.

The shrill ring of the telephone startles me. I walk to the kitchen, expecting the call that is becoming a ritual. I'm not too fond of it when he asks if everything is fine.

I place the receiver to my ear, about to say hello to the person who claims to love me more than life itself.

But the voice that greets me from the other side doesn't sound one bit like the man I have known for a while.

The hoarse voice over the phone calls me Klair Knox; the name is beginning to sound familiar to me. He says I had applied for a docent position at the museum some months ago and was wondering if I was available for an interview. I agree to the interview.

I'm not ready for a job, but having a job would be better than sitting around all day trying to remember a missing piece of my life.

I glance around for my cell phone after the caller hangs up. It's time for Luke to call, but for some reason, he hasn't called today. He is a busy man, being the director of a museum. I remember he told me the name of the museum. What was it again? Gevi?

Come to think of it, the caller said the position of a docent was for the same museum. If I get the job, will I be working with Luke every day? This new opportunity leaves me with a nostalgic feeling. Should I be happy or sad about this? I look for the large Georgian clock on the wall, its design a half-moon. I scoff at the fragmented design. It is a close depiction of what my memory is like now.

I walk into our living room, and a rag-looking carpet with bulb-like designs covers the floor. I reach my hand out to feel it on my skin. It's like a plain canvas with blotches from a paintbrush. I have asked Luke several times about them, but he is evasive about it. I might have gotten them on the night I had the accident.

Is this a reflection of me, or just another mirage of myself? I'm pulled from my daze by a loud clanging as the old clock and, its cuckoo birds make that annoying noise again. It's ten a.m. I sigh deeply, knowing what lies ahead. I must visit my therapist in thirty minutes. My husband and therapist are so desperate about what is in my head that I must see her every day.

Chapter Two

K^lair
This morning, I lie on a leather reclining couch in my therapist's office. My skin feels scratchy from the leather. I'm seeing my therapist, who is here to help, but for some reason, my palms feel wet, and it feels like I'm in an interrogation room.

"So, Klair, have you remembered anything?" my therapist asks.

I run my eyes along the edge of the window, which hangs above where she sits. A ray of sunlight streams into the room. She is seated behind a desk, which holds a nameplate showing her name: Dr. Abbey Mallot. Her curly hair seems a little messy, and her long-sleeved shirt is rumpled like she just woke up from bed.

Her awards hang on the wall next to the window. Although I have been here often, this room still looks strange, and I still feel uncomfortable; I don't know why.

I glance at a pinhole on the door of her office, and it reminds me of when I was little. I would peep through the pinhole whenever the property owner knocked on it, her voice loud with threats of eviction due to our unpaid rent.

"I'm ready when you are," my therapist says.

What is she ready for? For me to remember?

"Remember? What am I expected to remember? I can only retain a part of my memory of when I was twelve. I remember my mum's pale skin, her tired eyes, and the strong smell of alcohol. Every night, she used to take out my dad's photo from one of her lockers, staring at it for minutes. She would then cry heart-wrenching sobs that made me wish I could do something to end her misery."

My therapist touches the edge of her notepad and looks up at me.

"You must have been conflicted about your mother's feelings?"

"Conflicted? I remember my mum hiding her face between her elbows every time I walked in. She desperately tried hard to avoid me seeing her cry, but her sobs were enough to keep me awake in the middle of the night."

I turn my eyes at Dr. Mallot, being that it still feels strange in this room, but she doesn't look at me.

"Her curses, venting, and anger strangely resound in my head. Dad left us when I was twelve, never to return. The only memory I held of him was watching him on TV every night. I remember mum's words every time the nine p.m. news came up with the reporter, Dylan Knox. Mum would always raise her glass of drink to the TV, motioning to me while saying, 'Klair, that's your dad.'"

She touches her neck, and I notice a line that runs across her forehead. "Klair, you blink more often every time you speak about your mum. Have you realized that?"

"No, I haven't. Picturing the faces of the social workers who visited often is a memory I hate to recall."

On her table sits a small clock. I watch as its longest hand ticks away the seconds; it shows ten forty-five a.m. I'm glad I will soon be out of this office. I reach my hand towards my shoulder and rub it. I can feel goosebumps around my neck. This is how I felt every time the social workers frequented our one-bedroom apartment, more often than I can remember. After too many wails and the overpowering smell of hospital disinfectant, Mum was moved to an institution. And as for me, I got Mrs. Betty. During one of the visits, the social worker said, with a smile that seemed to fit the description of a smirk better, "Klair, your new home will be with Mrs. Betty. I promise you she is an angel. You will meet other kids like you and you will love it there." I bet Mrs. Betty was an angel who just happened to have lost her wings.

"How did you get out of that?" Dr. Mallot asks.

I snap back from my thoughts. I forgot I was speaking aloud and that someone was listening.

"Excuse me?" I ask.

"How were you able to get away from Betty's house?" She stares at me coaxingly, waiting for me to give her a response.

But I have nothing to give her. It's back to a blank page.

I blink my eyes several times in a row, trying to come to terms with what just happened. I unconsciously recalled something from years ago, which made me so excited. I smile at my psychiatrist, happy with my progress.

My happiness is short-lived as she continues staring at me intently. Oh... I remember I haven't given a reply to her question.

"I can't remember what happened after that. I'm sorry," I mumble.

"You don't have to be sorry, Klair. It will all come back with time. If you remember something before our next session, don't forget to put it down in the journal I gave you, okay?" She rolls her thumb between her fingers and then begins writing.

"Okay."

She bends towards her knee to pull a tread off her skirt. "Tell me about your morning, Klair. How did it go?"

For a minute, I do not know what to say. I do the same routine every day, never missing a step. I do it for my husband and the sheer lack of any other option most of the time. But this morning was a bit different.

I wonder if I should tell her about the flashes, the woman lying in a pool, the hallway I seemed to have seen somewhere, the headaches, the painting, the lonely feeling. Should I tell her about the reservations I have about my husband? I wonder if she would laugh at the absurdity or take me seriously.

"I saw flashes. A woman was lying in a sort of pool."

I watch her eyes light up in interest, and something else I can't seem to figure out. She moves her chair noisily closer to the table.

"What else did you see? What were you doing when this happened?"

"Everything else was hazy. My eyes were in and out of focus most of the time. And it gave me a nasty headache." I wrung my hands tightly in need of doing something.

"For patients with your case, the headaches are not novel. I would advise you to give yourself a break. Stop forcing yourself to remember anything. It will come naturally," she reassures me.

"But I didn't try to force it or anything. I was eating when it came."

For some reason, I decide to stick with that story. I know withholding the painting isn't helping with my treatment, but I do not want to share it with anyone. It is the only thing I have discovered without anyone spoon-feeding it to me. It feels like an achievement to me, one that I want to guard with my being. But against what exactly? This is insane.

"I got a job interview!" I say excitedly, expertly changing the topic.

"This is great news!"

"It's the position of a docent in the museum Luke works at." The name feels foreign as it rolls off my tongue, but I think it won't be long before I get used to it.

"And how do you feel about that? About working in the same place as your husband? About being out there in society?"

"I'm excited about it all. I know I don't have any previous memory of Luke, but I'm starting to rely on him. He is strong and hardworking. I can see why I must have fallen in love with him." I smile wistfully, not wanting to think about my reservations. Maybe everything is a figment of my frail imagination.

"And what about relating with other people? There will be a lot of tourists asking you for help and directions. You would act as a tour guide, leaving your harbor of refuge and going out without supervision.

Are you sure you can handle that, Klair?" She looks at me as if trying to see through me.

"Luke is going to be there. He won't let anything happen to me. And while acting as a tour guide, I will try to relate with the tourists because that is what I should be doing to get better. Interacting with people helps, right?"

"It sure does. Ensure you stay by Luke at all times. All the time."

I nod in response, admitting that I am too scared to wander around without Luke anywhere close by. I watch her write something in her notes.

"Is there anything else you would like to say before we wrap up this session?" She tidies her skirt as she gets up, prepared to walk me to the door.

"Klair?" A deep male voice breaks through the soft sounds of the air conditioner and the swishing of hands-on skirts. I obediently turn around, glancing up to see my husband glide in through the doors. He looks so dashing in his suit that I almost reach out to touch him. I keep my hands tightly by my side, unsure if Luke will like that.

I get off the seat as he walks toward me, taking me into his arms. He smells of coffee and newspapers like he always does each time he walks into our home from work. I wonder if I will smell that way when I begin working there.

Dr. Mallot watches us discreetly from where she stands, probably waiting for us to be done with our show of affection. She begins to walk toward us. I'm curious about what Dr. Mallot has written in her notes, but Luke is staring at me.

"Why are you here?" I ask, surprised to see him. He is usually not around for my sessions due to the nature of his job.

"I decided to come to pick up my favorite girl in the world. Is that a crime?" Luke asks with a boyish grin.

I can't help but smile back.

"You didn't call today. What happened?"

"I wanted to surprise you here. That call might have ruined it."

I do not see how calling would have ruined it, but I decide not to say anything about it.

"Klair made progress today," Dr. Mallot says, looking at Luke.

I don't appreciate how my therapist shares my session with Luke. I know I shouldn't feel this way since she is my doctor, and seeing her should help me recover, but I can't help it. She told me to only stick to Luke if I'm employed as a docent; this doesn't sit well with me, though it is as if she said it out of concern.

I walk some feet away from them. I glance at her note; it has the word *Clare*. Why did she spell my name wrong? Luke spells it *Klair*.

"She did?" Luke's question gets my attention; he turns to look at me with admiration in his eyes. "I am so proud of you."

I smile in response, wondering how fast the expressions in their eyes will change if I tell them I have no idea how I got a job interview or that I hadn't even applied in the first place. Luke doesn't know about the job yet. I shake my head, deciding not to say anything.

As if on cue, my stomach rumbles for lunch, and Luke holds out his hand, directing me out of Dr. Mallot's office.

Luke and I walk with Dr. Mallot to Luke's car. We make small talk about my progress report as we walk. Dr. Mallot suddenly stops, pivoting toward Luke, who is about to open the door for me.

"I need to run over some things quickly with you," she says, walking around to the back of the car.

Luke frowns at her, strokes his mustache, and then smiles at me apologetically.

"Get in, dear. This won't take long. I will be right back."

I observe as he walks to join her, wondering what they have to discuss that cannot be said with me there.

The feeling that something isn't right is coming back again, and I try to silence it. Luke loves me, and that's all that matters. Right?

Chapter Three

Klair

It has never occurred to me before, but as the gates open to welcome us back home, I feel the beginnings of panic in my chest. For some reason, I think the gates do more than welcome us in. It might be their huge and condescending look.

The way the gate attendant gapes at me gives me a churning feeling: it's like he knows things about me. I'm not just the resident who lives in block B, but something more.

I make a mental note to tell Luke about my feelings. Hopefully, he won't conclude that my feelings are imagined too.

Our daily routine doesn't feel any different today. I observe as Luke places some potatoes into the sink, turns on the faucet, and begins to wash them. He has always made the meals, never letting me get as far as even turning on the cooker. I have no idea why he does that. Is he just too caring, or is it something else? I try to read him with every move he makes as he cuts the meat and puts them into the pot.

Luke looks up at me and smiles. It seems he noticed my very studious eyes on him.

"Why?"

"Why what?" I decide to play the oblivious bride, as that is all left to do.

"Why were you staring at me that way?"

I shake my shoulders at his question; there is no way he will understand my thoughts. My husband is a mystery to me, and so is my life.

We do not seem to have much to talk about each time we are in the same space. I see a stranger, and so I should, considering I have no idea who he is, apart from the details he decides to tell me. I think he sees a highly mentally unstable wife with an imagination as creative as Da Vinci's paintings.

"You're sure nothing is wrong?" he questions, trying again to get me to talk. I contemplate obliging but decide not to. It is better to do that after he is done cooking.

Luke continues working in silence, unable to hide the fact that he is glad I'm not staring at him anymore.

We take the food out to the patio, watching the stars as we down the potatoes and meat, accompanied by a non-alcoholic beer I am unfamiliar with. I open my mouth several times as we munch, wanting to tell him what has been on my mind. But midway each time, I halt, deciding it is not the right time yet.

Thirty minutes and two empty plates later, I know I cannot keep quiet for much longer. I hold on to the hem of the fleece blanket covering my feet, hoping it will be able to grant me the warmth and relief I need as I open my mouth to speak.

"I got a call today for a job at the museum."

Luke has his head down, fully occupied by some article he is reading on his phone. He doesn't say a word. It's as if he doesn't hear me—or he's pretending not to.

"Can you hear me?" I ask, picking up the plates, to alert him of my presence more than to tidy up.

He looks up at me with a smile. Or not. I can't seem to decipher if it is a smile.

I study the lines that run across his face. Luke is a combination of classic rugged beauty, powerful sex appeal, and a passion for life. I love looking at him, but I sense he doesn't feel the same about me.

He closes the open tabs on his browser, still not looking at me.

"Honey, did you say something?"

I bite my lip, trying to debate between repeating the words or pretending I never said them in the first place. I can feel warm air escape my lungs, and it gives me a slight shiver.

I run my fingers through the soft fabric of the blanket, choosing to give it one more shot.

"I got a call today about a job at the museum."

"Oh, yeah!" he replies, his head gesturing along to his words.

He finally turns off his phone, taking his precious time to place it on the table beside him before looking up at me.

"Abbey told me about it."

"Abbey?" I raise my brow, gazing meaningfully at him.

I refer to my therapist as Dr. Mallot. Strangely, my husband just called her by her first name, as if he knew her personally. And his attitude about the news I just told him is very carefree. Too carefree.

He seems to have noticed his mistake, shrugging to cover up for the unintended slip. "Oh, Dr. Mallot."

He rises, takes the plates from me, and begins to step back into the house. Abruptly, he pauses midway.

"With your regular visits to the therapist and my frequent communication with her, I have naturally gotten comfortable with her. And, well, she doesn't mind it if I call her Abbey."

"She is still my doctor." I bite my lip. "You should keep it professional with her. It still feels like a better idea rather than getting all cool and casual with her. And what's there you have to talk about with her? I still can't remember a thing."

I stare at him, waiting for an answer, even though I know the question sounded rather like a statement. I hope she hasn't told him about the flashes; I wanted to keep that to myself.

He goes into the house, and I follow closely behind, wondering how long it is going to be until he comments on my employment status.

It isn't long.

"When is the interview?" he asks.

"Next Monday," I say.

"Are you ready for it?" He pads across the kitchen, doing the dishes and taking care of the remnants.

"Not really, but it's best to do something rather than sit around, trying to remember what doesn't seem to be available," I say.

He nods his head to my words, then turns off the lights in the kitchen, enveloping us in darkness. I get scared for a minute as the picture of the woman lying on the floor jumps at me from my memory. I haven't thought about it in a while.

"Luke?" I call out shakily, stretching out my hands blindly, trying to find him.

He finds me first, leading me out of the dark into the relieving lights of the big living room. I have this faint belief that he turned off the lights in the kitchen so I wouldn't make out the expression on his face. I know it is a baseless assumption, but I can't help it.

Luke snatches the car keys off the table, striding towards the door.

"I will be out for a couple of hours. You don't have to wait for me."

"Where are you going?"

"I want to go say hi to the guys."

Luke has two friends, and they like to hang out whenever they get the chance to. The last time Luke told me he was going to see them was a week ago, but I don't get why he is just telling me.

"So I should just allow you to stroll out the doors at this time of the night." I am inclined to say, moving closer to him. "Why not go see them tomorrow? It's safer and looks more responsible."

"Klair, I will be back before you know it. We are meeting at the hang-out that just opened around the corner."

"I don't want you drinking out there, and I know James might put you up to it. I don't like him."

James is a handsome man who wears his hair a bit too long and has a high endurance for alcohol. The times Luke has introduced us, he stared at me knowingly like he knows something I don't. And I'm not too fond of it.

Maybe he does know something.

"You used to like him, you know?" Luke responds in a low-down voice, trying to reason with me. "He was my best man at our wedding, and he also helped us in discovering this house."

"It isn't my fault I don't remember," I say.

"I am in safe hands, Klair. Go to bed."

He stalks off, not bothering to see if I am okay with it.

I walk into the room and stop by the canvas. I notice a covering on it, remembering vividly that it wasn't there the last time I attempted painting. It must be Luke. He doesn't allow any of the workers to get close to our bedroom. He says I didn't like it.

Maybe I had. Perhaps I took care of the space myself, decorating and arranging it as I pleased. At least then, I could tell the colors apart, deciding what shade went with the curtains. But I can't anymore, yet Luke still won't let the cleaners take care of it. He claims he doesn't want them messing with the décor. He says he wants the room protected.

Protected from what exactly? Protected from whom? It does not sit well with me. He cleans the whole room from top to bottom when he has the time. It turns out perfect each time he does that, but still, what is the essence of having workers come in all day if they can't clean up the room?

I slide onto the stool in front of the canvas, taking off the covering. It is a new paper. I can tell by the absence of the spontaneous strokes I made the last time. I don't know how long I stare at the plain canvas, but the bobbing of my head jerks me back to consciousness.

Luke is not going to like me falling asleep here.

I turn off the fluorescent lights and turn on the night lights. Sauntering to the bed, I brush the cat off the covers before getting in. A lot of thoughts go through my head as I try to sleep.

I wonder what it will be like working in the same place as Luke. Will he be protective as always, or will he treat me like a colleague there? I wish I had gotten something else, but I don't think I have any qualifications to get any other type of specialized job. Luke rarely talks about my education, and each time I bring it up, there is always a skillful way of brushing it off.

I guess I am fortunate even to have this interview in the first place. Did Luke put in a good word for me?

I hear the front door open. A few seconds later, I see the outline of Luke. I can smell the alcohol from where I lay. However, this state doesn't stop him from sighing out loud as he notices I forgot to turn off the bathroom lights.

He has told me many times, but it does not seem to stick to my already shitty memory, as I usually forget to turn that light off. I wonder why it irritates him when I do that. It doesn't take anything to turn off the lights himself, so why is he so worked up about it?

I stare at his outline for a moment, wondering if he is going to comment on my constant forgetfulness or not. I guess he decides not to, as he silently undresses before climbing in. His light snores begin a few minutes after his head touches the pillow.

I turn to gaze across at him, trying to get myself to remember if there was any form of romance between us before the accident. He always sleeps naked but has never made a move to touch me. He says we didn't have a child, that I didn't want to have one just yet. I want to have a child someday, but I hope it won't be Luke's. I don't know anything about his family, and I can't rely on him as a father to my child.

I fall asleep with that thought, my mind bringing a picture of what I believe happened that night.

Chapter Four

K lair

I wake up this morning and look in the mirror; a stranger's reflection is staring back at me.

Luke and my therapist say she is me, but she isn't me.

Her eyelids are sunken and teary. Her yearning eyes hold unknown weight as if she is looking for answers.

It's like the world has moved on, but she is left behind.

I don't know why I have this feeling. Everyone has answers, but all I have is questions about who I am.

I sigh; I walk into the room with the canvas. It seems like it holds my answers. I step on the floorboard, and it creaks.

I sit, reach for a paintbrush, and begin to paint. After a few strokes, all I have is an unfinished line. This room has a dewy smell with a fruity undertone, like a lump of dead meat. This smell has been here for a while. I spoke to Luke about it last time I smelled it, and he said it was from spoiled meat when our refrigerator malfunctioned. We have a new fridge now, but the smell is still here. I wonder what it's from.

He loves me, knows me, but I don't know him. I try to ask him about his family at times, but he is always evasive. Maybe he just doesn't like talking about them.

Maybe the interview at the museum, which I don't remember applying for, will give me answers to my unanswered questions.

"Klair!"

Luke is calling me. I turn on the faucet and begin to wash my hands; I don't want to tell him I was just staring into the mirror. His expression spells concern every time I do it.

I walk into the living room, where breakfast is on the table. I should say I'm lucky to have a man like him, cooking and doing the dishes every day, but I don't. I take a seat, then look at Luke, but it seems he is more interested in the sausage and eggs in front of him—or he is pretending not to notice my eyes watching him.

The sound of the TV pulls my attention, but it is inaudible: A man steps out of his car and shakes hands with two other men in front of the Monthel country's flag. It seems they are in front of the presidential house.

The man with a goatee mustache looks familiar, but everyone nowadays is familiar to me. On the screen, the headline reads:

Kultant, senate elects to visit the presidential house.

In my mind, I can't help but wonder what it will take to meet a president. Not that I want to meet him, but my mind nowadays is like a maze, with different exits and entry points, but I myself am stuck in it. I feel lost.

"Eat your food, Klair; you have an interview in thirty minutes," Luke says.

"He must be a powerful person," I say.

"Who?"

"Kultant, the man on the TV."

Luke types into his phone, a corner of his mouth twitches. He says, "Your food is untouched, Klair. It will get cold."

Chapter Five

K lair

"Good morning. I'm Ryan, the assistant art director of GAOM." A tall man walks into the room and takes a seat in front of me. My eyes glance to his right at a man with round rim glasses and short, shaved hair.

"This is David Will, the assistant curator with whom you will be working."

He gestures to his right, then to his left. And further adds, "This is Cindy Liam, the chief curator."

Cindy is skimming through what I believe is my resume—one I don't remember writing. Her eyes shine like diamonds, and in front of her are some documents she is writing on.

"Klair, tell us about yourself. Why do you think you are a good fit for the docent position with Gevi Museum of Art?" She flicks her pen back and forth between her thumb like she wants to be anywhere else but here.

I grip a strand of hair and tuck it behind my ear, trying to come up with words. I run my eyes to her left and notice a corner of Ryan's mouth widen.

Does he know me? Or is he just a nice man? That seems to be the most frequent question I ask myself nowadays every time I meet anyone. Do they know me? Could they give me a clue into my lost memory, which stopped when I turned sixteen at Betty's home?

I can feel my body relax.

Cindy asks again, "Why do you think you are a good fit for the docent position with Gevi Museum of Art?"

My mind reaches for my earlier memory while at Betty's, where I had to work twenty hours a week at a live theater parking lot. I also recall the research I did on the position the previous night to be prepared for the interview.

"The job of docent," I say, "is to guide the guests around the museum. The docent does not only guide by providing customer service to the guest, the docent is a part of the museum, so they must present themselves accordingly with its image."

"That sums up the role of a docent at Gevi Museum," Ryan says.

Cindy glances toward Ryan. "But she hasn't answered the question of why she will be a good fit for the position."

Ryan places his hand on the table. I look down at my shoes and then glance around the large room with five glass windows.

"I have a keen interest in art and believe my knowledge and appreciation for it will lead some guests who have never experienced art, to come to love it," I say slowly.

Cindy's forehead furrows. Ryan, who wears an air of relief, anchors his arms.

"I think she had the best response, Cindy." Ryan's eyes meet mine. He picks something like a pamphlet from the table and says, "Sometimes, your job might not involve more than providing service to the museum but will also mean assistance with inspecting, hanging the art, and getting the museum ready for the exhibits."

During the last words, he packs the sheets in front of him.

"Come with me." Cindy's voice snaps at me. "Do you have your documents? They need to be submitted to human resources so your pay rate and date can be confirmed."

We walk down a long hall.

"These are the exhibit halls," she says and points at the walls that have paintings on them. Beside the paintings are the names of the artists.

Down the hall, a younger girl with short curly hair is rushing toward Cindy. "Curator, we have a problem," the girl says.

"What is it, Sonia?" Cindy glances at her phone, which is vibrating. She takes it out and presses a button to mute it.

"Teri Hook's paintings just came back." Sonia places her palm over her face, then takes a few breaths. "They have mold on them, which they insist is from us."

"How can that be true, when there is a painting condition report from us when they borrowed the art?" Cindy asks Sonia, who shrugs her shoulders. "We will have to strip our storage, and inspect other paintings, just in case the mold came from us."

Cindy turns towards me. "Sonia is our intern and should be your tour guide around the museum, but your orientation will have to be moved to—" Her phone vibrates again, and she looks down at it and taps. "Can you be here on Wednesday at eleven a.m. instead?" she asks without looking at me but her phone, which she taps on. "I have a few calls to make."

"Sure, I can be here on Wednesday," I reply as she begins to walk away with Sonia.

I watch Cindy with fascination on the way; she seems busy and good at her job. She may have been mean to me at the museum, but it must have just been the work; it probably gets to people.

Then I think of Luke. I didn't see him at the interview. I glance around the hall towards the exit sign leading me down some stairs. This room is filled with sculptures, which I stand and admire for a while; before Luke's voice catches my attention.

Over the stairwell, which leads to the exhibit room, there is another stairwell. Luke is there with someone. I can see from the silhouette, that it is a man that Luke is talking to. Who is he?

"Have you been able to reach the new artist who submitted his art to the museum? We need him to sign the contract and we still don't have the piece with us." He motions, his hand pointed up, drawing an imaginary line into the air.

"We should display his art in the next exhibit which is in a month."

I want to say something, but for some reason, I decide to be silent and just listen.

"All I have is the anagram KK, which the artist used, and Deby met the artist for a face-to-face meeting before the accident. Deby must know who the artist is, but she is in a coma. If only Deby was awake," the guy beside Luke says.

Deby... I wonder who that could be and why Luke and the guy are talking about her. I watch Luke bring one of his hands to his ear.

"Cindy is doing great in her place, though; she is a great curator," Luke says. He turns around, glances and his eyes meet mine. Now, I can clearly see the guy standing beside him. It's Ryan from the interview. Luke taps him on the shoulder and heads toward me.

"Klair." The word comes from both men, almost in unison.

I notice that Ryan and Luke are of the same height, though Ryan has this laid-back aura about him. *Are they friends? Did Ryan know about me through Luke?* I wonder, pulling a strand of hair behind my ears.

I wave at them nervously and say, "Hi."

"Klair," Ryan says again. "Are you heading to the HR department?"

I shake my head. "No, Cindy said there is an emergency, and my orientation has been postponed."

Luke, with his hand in his pants pocket, looks toward Ryan and then at me. He asks, "Do you know each other?"

Ryan shakes his head as a gesture of disapproval. "I just met her to-day; she interviewed for the docent position. Klair, right?"

I nod.

"Yeah," Luke replies; he rubs his hand over his mustache while I glance at him. His sentence isn't complete. He is going to introduce me to Ryan as his wife, right?

"So, how do you know her, Luke?" Ryan turns towards Luke.

Luke glances at me, ignoring Ryan's question. "How was your interview?"

"Great," I say, nervously touching the strap of my bag. I'm hoping he will comment more on it, like he did about my progress at Dr. Mallot's office, but...

Luke glances at his phone again.

Ryan smiles and says, "Welcome to the team, Klair. Anyway, I have to go." He taps Luke's shoulder, then runs up the stairs. He reminds me of a free bird, unlike Luke, who is always serious.

I glance towards Luke, who is still skimming through his phone. I want to talk about the previous night; it seems I was too pushy when I mentioned my not wanting him to hang out with his friends. But without the memory loss, shouldn't I be worried like I was?

"Luke." I rub my hand with my other hand crossed over it. "About last night—" I continue, but he cuts me off.

"Your doctor's appointment today is at one, right?"

His words are a statement, not a question, but I shake my head.

He glances at his watch. "I will meet you at home by twelve forty-five p.m. and take you to the appointment," Luke says.

He walks closer to me and rubs my shoulder. It feels strange. Is he avoiding the topic or just doesn't care about it? Anyway, he is always patient with me, keeps up with my pace, and tries to work things out with me. He knows I have no memory of our ever being in love, which must be frustrating.

He knows everything I have planned for my day-to-day basis. It makes me feel fortunate since everything is new to me, but at the same time, he gives me this creepy vibe. It's like he has all his eyes on me—watching all my moves like a cat watches a mouse.

It's one p.m. and I'm seated in the office of Dr. Pearce, a neurologist I have been seeing since the accident.

"As I discussed with you several months ago, your examination result shows no abnormality to your eyes. Though your ophthalmologist said there is a positive finding of color blindness," Dr. Pearce, a plump old man with wavy hair begins.

He clicks his pen. "Which brings me to the question, how is your therapy session going with Dr. Mallot?"

A squeaky sound from the chair beside me pulls my attention towards Luke. He shifts in his seat. "Her sessions are going okay, though we are yet to see any progress." Luke's voice seems to quiver at the last words. I glance at him, and he rubs his right hand against his left. Is my husband nervous? About what and why? Is he worried about me because he loves me?

"The MRI result is clean, but your color blindness and amnesia are a particular case. Your therapist must have told you. The abnormality is psychological. It's your body's defense mechanism," Dr. Pearce continues.

I shake my head at his words, but it seems more confusing, so I ask, "Dr. Pearce, what do you mean by my body's defense mechanism?"

He rolls his pen between his thumb and finger. "In simple terms, Klair, it means that whatever you have forgotten is a trauma. Your body doesn't want you to remember it because it is trying to protect you."

"So, I shouldn't remember it, Doctor?" I ask. He is staring at me; he opens his lips, pauses, coaxes his brow, then says, "That's not what I'm saying, Klair. The thing is, everyone's defense system is different. For some, they go into the fight and some the fright." He places his hand on the table. "In simple terms, you might overcome this trauma, or it might affect your ability to cope with your normal daily activities."

"So, Dr. Pearce, I shouldn't try to remember, should I?" I begin, but I can feel Luke's sweaty palm over mine; he cuts me off.

"Like you mentioned, Doctor, I guess she should take her time to remember rather than rush to... because it might lead to a breakdown."

He reaches into his pocket and brings out a handkerchief. "Klair, your therapist will be in the right position to discuss this with you." He dabs his face.

"Okay, Doctor." Luke stands up from his chair. "Should we schedule the next appointment?"

"Sure, Luke, and you have my number, so if you have any concerns, call me."

Luke and I walk out of the doctor's office and down the hall leading to a nursing station, where one of the nurses is busy typing into a computer hung against the wall. The other nurse is on the phone, her hand directing a staff member towards something.

I glance at the nurse who is typing; her fingers type in the name Deby Williams. The name seems familiar, more than anything has this whole week, so I stare. My mind begins to run through a lot of questions about who the name belongs to and where I've heard it before. Oh, it's the name Luke and Ryan mentioned at the museum.

I can feel a tight grip on my wrist; it pulls me away. In a flash, I see two men rush past me with a stretcher. A voice calls to me.

"Klair."

I turn around towards the force that pulled me. It's Luke.

"You need to be careful," he says in a tone filled with concern.

"I'm sorry, I don't know what happened back there," I say.

I turn toward the nurse, but she is gone.

"Wait here, let me get the vehicle from the valet," he says, then walks away. The name Deby Williams begins to play like a broken clock repeatedly. Did I know this name and who she was?

Chapter Six

K lair

Think, Klair. What's the last thing you remember? Focus.

I place my hand against my waist and give my mind time to think. I imagine all my memories twirling towards me like a tornado.

Nothing...

I focus again, and then I remember my session with Dr. Mallot. I remember that I spoke about my mother—how she was sad about my dad leaving us and how I was separated from her and she was institutionalized. Where is she now?

I bite my lip, confused. I should have gone to see her after I remembered, but I didn't. Why? Being that she was my mother, she should know more about me than I know about myself, right?

"So, what do you think?" someone asks. She is assertive, but I ignore her words.

I should have thought of going to my mum for answers but, of course, nowadays I barely think probably because Dr. Mallot's daily sessions haven't happened in three days.

Sometimes I imagine Dr. Mallot as a puppeteer and myself as a puppet; she tells me what to remember and what I shouldn't. I picture her sticking a surgical knife into my brain, trying to dissect and check for whatever is in there. I shiver from the thought and break into sweats. I feel relieved that I don't have to see her.

She called this morning, but like the last two days, I have rescheduled using work as my excuse. This job is a blessing.

After all, Dr. Pearce had mentioned I shouldn't put pressure into remembering, though Luke looked very uneasy that day. It's like he doesn't want me to remember, or maybe it's just me living in my head.

"So, what do you think?" It is that assertive voice again. I turn around and notice that I'm in a room. The room feels warm, and around me are chattering voices. Sonia is speaking to a guest while gesturing at a painting on the wall. I look ahead, and a woman with spectacles is standing there; she is wearing a dress with a cardigan and a scarf around her neck. She has something in her hand: a handkerchief? A hand fan? She is staring at something. I trace the line of her gaze; it's towards the wall, at a painting—one I have been standing in front of, lost in my thoughts. Is she on the phone? Is she talking to me? Now I am staring at the painting.

She asks again, "So, what do you think?"

"About?" I glance at her. "The painting?"

I gesture at it. I am a docent, so wouldn't it be obvious that she is asking for my input on the painting?

My lips are dry, and I swallow. I can't find the right words. An irony, right? A colorblind person works with these mediums that allure color. Paintings are artistically brought to life by an artist's stroke on the canvas. The colors give it life and meaning; it helps their creative imagination to be seen and understood by whoever views their pieces. I can't see color, but this woman is asking for my thoughts on this piece in front of me.

Having this job might not have been a blessing after all. I rub my sweaty hands against my shirt. Luke's hands at the doctor's office were sweaty too. Is he nervous about something? I glance at her again, and she is still staring at the painting. I look back at the piece again; it reminds me of my skin every time I look in the mirror.

I say, "It's a blotch."

She begins laughing, opens the fan in her hand, and covers her mouth with it. Still laughing, everyone is beginning to stare at her, then me. Cindy is walking toward us, and I'm more nervous than ever.

"A blotch indeed," the woman says and continues to laugh hysterically.

My hands are sweatier than before. What should I do? I just got hired. Would I be fired this soon?

Cindy walks toward me and says, "I'm sorry, Teri."

I can feel that Cindy hates me already, maybe for my incompetence. I could sense it from the first day I met her, but I am happy to see Cindy intervene. "How can Ryan expect someone with color blindness to be a docent? Beats my imagination," she mentions in a low voice but loud enough to attract a few glares. "No one listens to me." She curls her lips.

Some of the guests are now openly staring at us. I'm ashamed. Cindy knows, and Ryan too, but how? Luke? I rub my hands against my skirt, still staring at her, but she doesn't look at me. She gestures to Sonia to come over instead and adds, "You should have worked as a museum assistant instead, but no one will listen to me."

Teri closes her fan, and she isn't laughing anymore. "Cindy, I love her. She is different from everyone here." She looks around. "They are all so uptight, like they don't use the restroom. They walk with their heads up like other people are under their feet." Teri touches her shawl. "Sometimes I just want to say to them, 'Look down, there is a grenade coming your way.'"

Teri's dry joke isn't funny to me; however, Cindy covers her mouth with her hand and laughs.

Teri taps me on the shoulder and says, "I was in a dark place when I painted this piece. That's why I titled it *Drown*."

Sonia is coming towards us; she is smiling, and, in her hand, she has something: I think it's a flyer. She looks and then whispers something. Cindy's eyes brighten, then she looks at Teri and says, "Your painting, *Beloved*, has sold."

"No, Cindy, that piece was only for exhibition; I don't want to sell that one," Teri replies. She and Cindy walk away.

Sonia says to me, "Cindy wants you to work as the museum assistant for today's exhibit."

I nod, then wonder if she also knows that I'm colorblind.

I am standing at the front desk. A tall man with curly hair walks toward me and smiles. The same question I have been asking a lot runs through my mind, but this time I hold it back. Of course, he doesn't know me. I smile.

"Thank you for visiting Gevi Art Museum. Today we have an exhibition titled, *My Story.*"

I shake my head; it's just me and my imagination. I reach for one of the museum's flyers and hand it to him, but he isn't leaving. Instead, he stares.

"Klair Knox?" he asks.

"Can I help you?" I ask.

He raises his eyebrow as I'm about to repeat the question. I guess I still haven't gotten tired of it. Maybe someone will tell me one of these days: Of course, you are not the woman who woke up one day to learn that you are married and have a cat, which you hate its sight alone and are still not sure you ever loved it.

He points at my nametag and smiles. "Beautiful name. I know someone with the same name." He places his hand in his pocket and looks down. When he looks up again, his chin seems red, and he is smiling. "I did not know that name was so common."

I sigh in disappointment. He is still looking at me as I raise my head and look at him. He is staring at the oversized ring on my finger. I can feel my ring fall, so I adjust it on my knuckle.

He says, "I should have been here to get the details of wall background and lighting that will be used in the area of my exhibit showcase, but I got the news about the exhibition at the last minute."

"Oh, you are an artist?" I ask, my eyes brightening.

He nods. "Yeah, I am a photographer, and my work, *SHE*, is one of the featured pieces for my story."

"You will have to talk to Cindy about that," I say. "She is the chief curator, so I will take you to meet her."

I excuse myself, and the two other museum attendants take over helping the next customer. He is still staring at me and making me nervous. I see Cindy from afar. I don't want to lock eyes with her again.

"That's the curator," I say and point toward her.

"Which?" he asks. I see him look ahead. "What color is she wearing?"

He is making me nervous again. It's like I need colors to do everything, even helping a guest meet the curator. I sigh and gesture towards Cindy again, saying, "She has her hair tied into a bow."

I'm about to walk away but I look at his face, and the thought of the other Klair crosses my mind. I bite my lips for the courage to begin. "About the other Klair Knox. Where is she from?"

He stares in silence. I haven't replied to his question about what color Cindy is wearing.

Cindy knows about my impairment. Can I just tell this stranger about it? He might know something. "It might sound strange, but everything has been strange for a while, for me anyway. I can't see colors. The doctor says my impairment is not physically or chemically affected. He calls it a special case because it's psychological."

He is staring again, and I trail his eyes to the wall behind me. He says, "You don't need to show me to Cindy. That's the curator's name, right?"

On the wall is a photography piece, I can't see the color, but it's a woman: a ballerina.

"She is beautiful," I say.

He points at the piece. "Klair Knox—she inspired the piece. I wanted to capture beauty, art, strength, and the agile ballerina: a phantom with all these abilities." He touches the piece. "I like where it's hanging, and the background is perfect."

"Cindy is good at her job," I compliment. At first, I debate but end up asking, "She must be beautiful. Klair, I mean. So, what's your story?"

A wisp of a smile runs across his face. "Yeah, she is. She inspired me to become a photographer because I was blind once."

"I'm so sorry about that," I say.

"My parents and I were going to my aunt's birthday. There was an accident, which led to my parent's death and partial blindness to my eyes." He takes a deep breath and then continues. "I met a girl at the hospital during my stay. She was thirteen years old and I was twelve, her name was Klair Knox and her mum was also there at the hospital. We became friends, and one day, I told her I wished there was a way I could make this moment last forever."

He looks at the exhibit hall before continuing. "At that time, I was beginning to forget what my dad and mum looked like, so it was very saddening for me." He places his hand in his pocket and changes his posture. "Klair suggested I should become a photographer because it keeps memories alive for a long time."

"She was a smart girl," I say.

"Yes, she was," he replies. "She once said to me, 'Pictures tell our stories. With it, people can see our expression and embrace what we feel.'"

I could feel a little jealousy on hearing his story because I still didn't know if Luke and I had a story and a beautiful one like theirs.

I ask, "Did you guys get married?"

He shakes his head. "We were separated. Her mother was institutionalized, and she was sent to an orphanage. I, on the other hand, went to live with my aunt." My heart jumps, his story strikes a resemblance to mine, about her name and her mother being institutionalized, but if he knew me, he wouldn't be telling me about her, right? Instead, he would have said it's about me. I know I faintly have my past memory, but I don't think I know this man.

"That's sad. I hope you meet her again someday."

"Klair..."

Someone is calling, and I know the voice. I'm having a great conversation with this stranger, but Cindy, just like Aunt Betty, sure knows when to rub salt into my open wound. My fist is tightening as I look up. She is standing in front of me and the stranger, whose name I still don't know.

"Kai Beck?" Cindy reaches her hand out, and he shakes it. "We have been expecting you since yesterday evening."

"I was told about the exhibit at the last moment," he replies.

Cindy looks at the wall behind me. "Are you satisfied with where your piece is?"

"Yes, the background color is very subtle, yet I can feel the exuberance I was trying to capture," he replies. "And, I also have a great docent beside me," he adds.

Cindy looks at the printed sheets she is carrying and says, "Your piece has received a lot of positive reviews, and our gallery would love to do a special exhibit with your work alone. Would you be interested?"

"Special exhibit? But I'm a new artist," Kai replies.

"Let's just say that there is a collector who has taken much fondness for your piece and she is an important sponsor for our museum."

"I will have to talk to my agency about it," he replies.

Cindy turns towards me. "Klair, could you find Sonia, please? She will let you know what your next task is."

I want to argue because I want to stay longer with the stranger to finish hearing his story, but Cindy is the chief curator and can order anyone around. So, I leave to find Sonia.

At home, I take out my color palette. I feel this is the only thing my body understands that I am good at, though I have no memory of ever painting. I study the canvas that sits on the easel. I think of the incident at the museum with Teri, then Cindy, and I can feel a slight pain around my neck. Hot air begins to rise towards my chest, and tears begin to form in my eyes, but why?

I think of the man at the museum and then wonder about the other Klair and what she was like. I wish I had heard the whole story, but Cindy had sent me to a loading dock where painting for the new exhibit had arrived in Calitain. The man was gone when I returned. His story about Klair's mother being institutionalized feels familiar, but I don't think he knows me.

I'm crying. Is it because of the man's story, which isn't mine, or because Cindy and Ryan know of my impairment? I feel betrayed.

I dip the brush into one of the colors, though not aware of what color it is, then bring my hand towards the canvas. I draw a stroke, a line perhaps. My hand begins to shake as I am being pulled into a trance. In it, my hand covers my eyes, and bright light floods me. I see a woman; she is carrying something. What is it?

"Klair. Klair." Someone is calling me. It's a familiar voice: Luke. My hand feels weak, and the brush falls out of it. I'm out of the trance, and Luke is standing in front of me.

"Klair," he calls again. "Are you okay? Are you having those flashes again? Have you told Abbey about them?"

I look at Luke, my eyes burning. I hear a clatter and see the canvas on the floor beside the brush with its bristles looking worn out. It mocks me. Luke reaches for the floor and picks something up: it's my ring. "Sorry, Klair, I forgot to resize this. I have been busy at work," he says.

"Of course, you were."

I pick up the brush as he walks closer to me, he rubs my shoulder and says, "Please don't be angry; I promise I will resize it." Resize: is it so easy? Does everything become okay just because it has been resized?

"You told Cindy and Ryan that I have an impairment. Did you stop at the color blindness, or did you add my memory loss to the soup to give it more flavour?"

He looks upset. He stares at me and then says, "Honey, are you off your meds because you have been working? Should I schedule you to see the doctor?"

"What?" I stare at his pursed lips, the expression on his face. What is it? I can't read it. I'm taken aback. I was beginning to know this man, but I don't know him.

His words sound like concern, with a spice of sarcasm. I watch him plate our food. In my mind, I try to think about what happened to me that night. Where is my mum? I know she was institutionalized, but I can't recall where. It seems Luke will not tell me where she is either.

Every time I raise the topic, he tells me it would be better if I recover before I look for her, and I wonder why. Do I need to search the house for anything that can lead me to where my mum is? She must know the truth about that night, about Luke, and everything.

If she is still at an institution, I'm sure it has monthly institution fee. From the little I remember, she was not staying there for free. Who do I talk to?

"Five dollars for your thought," Luke says.

His eyes glint, but from what? I stare how his hands move as he plates our food, the way he slightly rests his head over his shoulder, then smiles.

He seems happy about something. We set out to eat, but he keeps glancing at his phone like it holds something; I don't know. He is usually uptight. This Luke is strange.

"Is everything okay?" I ask.

"Yeah. The guys just texted me." I can feel the skin on my face tighten. By guys, he means his friends. He tells me about hanging out with them at the last minute. He always does this.

"Are you guys hanging out?" I ask.

Luke shakes his head in affirmation, his eyes still fixed on his phone screen.

"Honey, I won't be long."

He has never been long whenever he spends time with his friends. He usually returns before midnight, but why do I have this eerie feeling? Why does it feel like Luke is lying or hiding something from me?

An earlier thought crosses my mind. Searching the house when he leaves will be a great start towards finding the truth, but how about what Luke is hiding from me? I think it will be best to find that out tonight.

I pretend to take a bite of the food and watch him walk into the bathroom. I run outside towards his large pickup truck, jumping into the back of it, and wait for Luke. My petite frame works in my favor, though I pray he will not have anything he needs to take out of my hiding space. I pray he will not see me through his rearview mirror. I pray he wouldn't hear my heartbeat or breathing.

Luke turns on the car's ignition, and the car accelerates into the distance. I don't know where he is going. The road is so unfamiliar. Soon the car comes to a stop, and I watch him step out, then I carefully follow suit.

An intense smoky smell fills the night air as if something's burning. I throw my cardigan over my head for disguise, though I can feel the cold wind brush through my hair.

I rub my hands over my shoulders as my eyes notice the tall building with bright lights and loud sirens. This place is familiar.

I have been here with Luke before. The same hospital where I saw the name Deby. Why is Luke here at this time of the night? I quietly follow him down the hall until a hand pulls me.

Chapter Seven

K lair
     Shhh...

I can feel a hand over my mouth and hear a thumping heartbeat. Is it mine, or is it the stranger's? He is pulling me closer, and through the little curtain, I can see Luke. He is talking to a nurse. What is he saying? Who is this stranger behind me? His scent is intoxicating with a hint of citrus.

He says again, "Shhh... Klair, Luke is outside."

My heart is thumping louder. He knows my name.

"What were you thinking, leaving the house, Klair?" the stranger asks.

"Who are you? How do you know my name?" I ask, but I can see Luke and a nurse coming towards the room.

The stranger pulls me closer to himself, and we hide in the little curtained area of the hospital room.

"As I said, Mr. Mallot, she had seizures this evening and was transferred to the ICU where she is being monitored. We ran a few tests on her to determine the cause of her seizures, which might be due to her electrolytes, but we should know for sure by the time the results come back," the nurse says while walking into the room with Luke. My heart jumps, and my foot slides back a little as I lean closer to the stranger.

The nurse called him Mr. Mallot. Is that his last name? I don't know much about his family, but Luke shares the same name with my therapist?

"Did anyone come to see her today?" Luke asks the nurse.

His voice sounds different from the one I know. I can see from the curtain that it's just him and the nurse in the room. His strange, baritone voice is making me shiver. It seems I live with a voice actor. Who are they talking about, and who was he expecting to visit? The stranger behind me?

"No," the nurse says. "We notified you, the emergency contact on her face sheet," she adds.

"Okay, keep me updated," he says.

The two of them leave the room, and the stranger's hand lifts off my mouth. I turn around to see the stranger; his laid-back feel and eyes which hold warmth, staring at me.

He asks in a soft tone, "What do you remember?"

My brow is furrowing, and my eyes are narrowing. I then remember that if Luke gets home before I do, I won't have any excuse, so I muster up the courage to say, "Sorry, I have to go. Luke is my ride."

I quicken my pace, my pulse rises, and questions rush towards me. Who was Luke visiting at the hospital? His mum, whom he doesn't like to talk about? I don't know if he is an orphan or just estranged from his family. I haven't met anyone yet. Was it perhaps my mum? If it were my mum, Luke would tell me she is sick, right?

I climb back into the truck and wait for Luke. He finally turns on the ignition, and the car accelerates into the night. The vehicle bounces, and then I sense an earthy smell.

This drive is different from when we go home. It is longer. The car comes to a stop, and in the distance, a passing train whistles. I wait for Luke to step out of the car, and then take a peek.

From the back seat, I can only see a little. There is a flashing light in the distance and a passing train next to it. Luke reaches into his pocket and places something in between his lips. The clicking sound of a lighter follows.

Smoke escapes into the air. My husband is smoking. Luke never smokes!

I want to push open the door and walk towards him, but to say what? Am I the unbearable wife who makes her husband leave the house and drive this far to smoke?

Soon, I spot a figure coming out of the woods. It is headed towards Luke. At first, I think to warn him, that he might be in danger from the figure. All I have to do is tell him I understand and accept him smoking. I don't remember ever telling him I hated it, though.

I shake my head and glance for Luke. As I do, a loud giggle echoes into the night. He opens his arms and lets the figure run into them.

A sharp pain runs through my heart. I can feel hot air around my chest. I swallow hard; my hand clings to the headrest of the driver's seat. My eyes begin to feel watery.

I glance over to Luke, a beam of light from the train tracks giving me a little glimpse of her long flowing hair. It rests over her hips. Her hands wrap around his neck, and he twirls her around. I cover my ears to her loud giggle, which even the sound of the train can't overshadow.

They are talking, and it feels like hours have gone by. I stare into the quiet night, and gaze into the stars, but they hold no beauty. The chirping sound of the crickets in the night keeps me company.

Will they be here all night? What exactly are they talking about? He kisses her, and they are hugging.

I look away; I can feel pain run through my heart. The chirping sound of the car's remote brings my attention back to Luke. He is walking towards the car.

I hide myself and the door slams shut.

The strong smell of cigarettes and the moth-like scent lingers in the car. He whistles and starts the car.

I'm cursing under my breath through the drive. I wish I could tape his lips so he could drive in silence. The car pulls into a driveway, and all I want is to hide under my sheets and cry; but on a bed shared with Luke, I swallow my tears.

This morning, a loud clang from that damn wall clock wakes me from sleep, not that I could sleep anyway. I can feel this unbearable pain in my forehead. I try to recall the memory from last night.

Mr. Sims jumps on my bed, his paw outstretched towards my hair. His tail waggles, and he walks over my head. I can feel it coming—the watery eyes, the sneeze, then the itchy throat. My allergies keep flaring when he is around, yet my husband says I loved him.

I begin to cry. From the allergies or from what happened last night, I can't tell. I can hear Luke's footsteps. He is coming into the room. As usual, he is up from bed before me.

The squeaking sound of the door and the clanking sound of the clock come at the same time. Luke is at the door; he is staring at me. I wipe my eyes.

"It's six a.m. Klair." He walks towards the window. "You are going to be late," he says.

I watch him lean against the wardrobe. He is fiddling with something. What is he reaching for? He brings out his socks and stares at me, but I look away and speak. "Luke, I don't feel too good. I will take a taxi to work," I lie.

The truth is, I don't want to be in the same car with Luke this morning. I can feel nausea rush through me. I jump out of my bed, plunge towards the floor, and let it out into the toilet. I'm crying again.

"The money is on the table," Luke says. He is indifferent to my emotional outburst.

I turn on the faucet and wash my face. I see my reflection in the mirror: my bulging eyes with drippy mascara. I must have forgotten to wipe my makeup off after I returned yesterday.

I am crying. I let my heart's content pour. I can feel this pinching pain run through me. My throat still feels like it is about to close. An unknown number is calling, and I pick up. My taxi is waiting outside the house.

I can't concentrate at work this morning, still thinking about last night. I haven't seen Luke today, but I keep staring at every woman around me. Who is she, the woman with the long hair? Light like a feather, who clung onto Luke. I think about how he freely twirled her around.

I walk into the breakroom and take a seat. Sonia walks in; she says nothing to me but begins to brew herself a cup of coffee. I stare at her hair as I decide her short hair is probably a wig. Her natural hair is longer. Every woman I see today feels like the woman at the train track—they all have natural, long hair.

I'm painting a picture of her and Luke in my head. Cindy walks in. She is talking to Sonia, but all I can think of is the mystery woman.

Someone else has walked in; he is talking to Sonia and Cindy. They are laughing.

"Would you like some tea?" he asks.

Did Luke ever love me? I wonder to myself. Should I tell him I know about the other woman? If I do, how will he react?

"Would you like some Jasmine tea?" he asks again. He is talking to me. He taps me on the shoulder. I look up.

"Ryan!" I say with a gasp.

He smiles. I can see Sonia whispering something to Cindy from the corner of my eyes. They walk out, and I look over to Ryan again. He places a cup of tea in front of me.

"How are you holding up, Klair?" He takes a seat in front of me. "I know the job must be very demanding, but I have received a lot of compliments from the guests. They love you, Klair."

I doubt that Ryan is telling the truth, and I am still wondering if Luke told him about my color blindness.

"Teri Hook wants you to assist her with the next exhibit," Ryan says.

"But..." I begin. I want to mention the elephant in the room. "Luke must have told you about..." I hold back my words and look at him.

He is staring at me, too; in his eyes, I can see warmth. He gestures to me to sip my tea.

"It will get cold, Klair."

I take a sip of the tea. I shake my head because something feels different. I take another sip, glance at Ryan, and ask, "What tea is this?"

"It's Jasmine," he says.

The smell is familiar to something. What? I think the scent, in the car when Luke came in. The other woman's smell.

I sigh, and something feels different from the tip of my tongue. The tea has a clean taste, unlike the Jasmine tea Luke makes at night, one with a mold-like bitter aftertaste. I can feel my heart race. I look at Ryan again and ask, "Are you sure this is Jasmine tea?"

He nods his head, affirming his words positive. I can feel my palms begin to sweat. I rub them against one another.

"You know, don't you?" he says.

"Know what?" I ask, but he stares at me. I look away, and then I ask the one question I have been wanting to ask him. "Ryan, what were you doing at the hospital last night?"

He set his cup on the table quickly. I can hear the teacup clank against the saucer. Ryan places his hand over the table and looks at me. "Klair, what do you remember?"

"Nothing, Ryan." He is still a stranger to me. Can I confide in him about anything, such as my mum's whereabouts? And Luke's last name? For all this while, I should have come to him earlier. I should have laid my cards all out and told Ryan everything; if I did, he might have the answers I was looking for. I touch the brim of the cup like it holds the courage I need.

"What do you know, Ryan?" I ask. It's best I lay that out. From the moment I walked in for the interview, I had this feeling that he knew something.

"The truth, Klair, is that I have questions too, but does the name Deby sound familiar?"

Deby is the name Luke and Ryan mentioned. It's the same name I saw the nurse at the hospital type into the computer. Should I disclose this little information to him when I really don't trust him?

"What about her?"

"The woman at the hospital is Deby, and she was in an accident." He sets his cup on the table.

"In an accident?" My eyebrow rises a bit. I, too, was in an accident. "What type of accident?"

"I'm not sure, Klair, but she came to see you. The rest is just a blur to me."

"She came to see me? Why?" I ask, but someone walks into the room. Ryan turns towards me.

"Klair, let's talk more in my office."

Chapter Eight

R^{yan} Today is May 17, 2022. It's been eight months since the incident which led to Deby being medically pronounced comatose. I run my eyes around the room for the wall clock; it's eight p.m. and Klair should be in the hall.

I must speak to her. I know we said last time, but it still feels like she is holding something from me: a secret, perhaps.

Placing my hand against the table, I come to a stand, but something catches my attention. My desk has a reading lamp and, in its center, stacks of documents waiting for my signature. It has been a busy season, especially with the upcoming exhibit *Wedding Bells in December* and the museum's plan towards mechanizing gifts for the guests in attendance. These files will remain on my to-do list for now.

I begin to brew a cup of vanilla-flavored coffee. I hear the dripping sound, and its black content fills my cup, but I just can't get Klair out of my head.

Klair's question about the incident keeps playing in my mind. I'm as clueless as she is about it.

Thoughts fill my mind about the morning of Saturday, August 18, 2021...

I had just woken up and was about to go on my jog when Deby Williams, the previous docent of Gevi Museum, called me in an ecstatic voice.

"Ryan, she is a genius."

I could feel the hesitation to ask her who "she" was. I placed my hand on the living room table beside me.

"Deby, can you at least tell me what you are up to? I know you said it's confidential and this person wants to remain anonymous, but…" I asked. I took a deep breath. "It feels like I am being left in the dark."

I could hear Deby remind me once again that I would be debriefed on the issue at the right time. After she ended the call, I anxiously stared at my phone throughout that day. I was curious about the informant's identity and the information she was going to disclose to us.

Deby never called that Saturday evening after the supposed meeting with the informant, whose name she never disclosed. This made me nervous; it was like she was running a special intelligence mission.

Around seven the following morning, I called Deby's phone, only to be told by the nurse at St. Patrick's Hospital that they were looking for the patient's family. Deby, according to the nurse, had no identification. Her phone was locked, and the only call that came in was mine that morning. The nurse continued that Deby had been transferred to the hospital due to what seemed like a hit-and-run accident and the police were notified.

How did it happen? Even the police say the case is under investigation. By jumping through some hoops and a favor from a friend, I was able to get her artifacts—the items she had with her during the accident. There were two canvases that I believe held the answer to who she was meeting that day.

January 11, 2022

I think the police kept her artifacts for too long, but I finally made a breakthrough six months after the accident when the police finally released her items.

Cindy had cleared the space Deby used at the museum after she replaced her, which led to me finally retrieving Deby's things from her previous desk. I'd have gotten them sooner, but the position was left open for a while with the hope of Deby returning. And the police took their time releasing it.

Among her things, I found one of her notes with the name Klair Knox and a line drawn across it. Along with the note was an art piece with the anagram KK. I assume it is the same piece Luke mentioned he wants hanged at an exhibit. I still haven't told him I have the piece.

It could have just been a coincidence that the anagram could be interpreted as the name Klair Knox, but I had nothing else to rely on but this new clue, so I began to run an investigation on the name. To my amazement, I found out she is married to the art director of Gevi Art Museum. He has always been a sketchy character to me, especially when it came to his evasive response to questions.

Before the incident—I mean Deby's—I noticed a discrepancy in the account, so I raised a question to Luke. He was very indifferent about it. I even thought I made too much a deal out of it until Deby came to me about the same issue.

Deby and I began to investigate, but then there was an informant who was about to disclose something to Deby about Luke, the art director. I remember that Deby had two canvases. Finally, the answers I had been searching everywhere for.

I cursed under my breath when I unveiled them: two plain canvases; behind one of them, the name: Kultant. It didn't relate or sound familiar to anything.

The anagram solidified my suspicion towards Klair, who, upon deep investigation, I found out was a painter. Disappointment hit right through me. She lost her memory of her identity and the truth about what happened that night.

She could be faking it. After all, Deby mentioned the informant wanted to stay anonymous. I had to get closer to her, but how? I needed the answer to what happened to Deby, but no one had it.

After the accident, I drove to the address I found attached to Deby's artifact, and there I saw Luke and Klair comfortably enjoying their evening out. Before Deby's accident, I had been to Luke's place for a celebration of some sort. If I can remember well, it was in a different part of town. If Klair is married to Luke, why is the address different? What am I missing?

Anyway, raising the topic about his wife's accident, which I knew would connect to Deby's accident, wasn't even a question. I could have spooked him about the investigation, but maybe he already knew, which would explain why Deby is hooked to a respirator at the hospital. The guy is very shady. He must have been involved in the accident. The artifact had to be important evidence, but without more, I couldn't ask him what happened to Deby and his wife.

Luke assumed the role as responsible party for Deby's care. None of her family members could be contacted. He took responsibility for her financially, though my instinct tells me it's because he wanted to be there whenever she woke up.

March 23, 2022

I had just finished my duties for the day when a light tap came on my office door. Sonia walked in.

I nearly jump out of my seat when she said the exact words I heard from Deby eight months ago, before the incident.

"Ryan, there is a discrepancy on the account records."

I stood up immediately and closed the door behind Sonia. I deliberated between asking her for help and telling her what I knew. We soon talked about it. Sonia introduced the idea of having Klair work at the museum.

"But how can we get her to work here? We have no idea if she has any experience for working here." I asked Sonia.

She shook her head at my words, then replied, "How about a docent?"

"A docent?" I coaxed my brow; I could feel my fingers tap against the glass table in my office. The idea was nerve-racking. Neither of us knew who she was, so that was a risk.

"What about a resume?" I threw in the question because of my hesitation.

Sonia gave me a mischievous smile, then said, "It's an entry-level position, so HR won't go into many checks, and with my name or yours in the recommender, she will be accepted."

"How about her husband? He might know she never applied!" I questioned.

"That's the tricky part, but we can't just sit around, Ryan," Sonia replied.

We placed the idea into action, and it worked. I was ecstatic when I walked into the interview room and finally put a face to the name, but who could have thought that it would be yet another disappointment with her at the museum? She had lost her memory.

Chapter Nine

K lair

I lay on my bed tonight. I can feel the heat gush through my window. The AC is broken, or did Luke lie about it being broken? Nowadays, I can't trust anything that he says.

I toss and turn while he is sleeping soundly. I stare at his bare chest and can almost see her long nails run through his hair.

I wonder why he sleeps so comfortably with me beside him. It's like my body exhumed his testosterone. It's just a thought; after all, I wouldn't be able to stand his filthy hands touching my skin.

I want to wake him up. I want to ask him about her. How long was he planning to keep this from me?

I spring to my feet and head for the bathroom. I seem to do that a lot these days.

I turn on the faucet and fill my hands with cold water, splashing my face with it, then stare in the mirror. Why am I even jealous? Did I ever love this man?

I was afraid to go back to bed. There is a stranger beside me.

I think about my meeting with Ryan at the hospital, then at the break room. I think about his question: what do you remember?

What do I remember? Nothing. Please, does anyone care to fill me in, to share a few pieces of myself that don't feel like me?

I have no strength in my legs, so I slump into the couch. Luke is awake now; I hear his feet drag against the floor. The bathroom door shuts. What is he doing in there? Probably calling her in the middle of the night while he thinks I'm asleep. No, I couldn't think like that. I'm becoming paranoid these days.

I walk towards the room with the canvas, shutting the door behind me as I go inside. I sit in front of a canvas; it feels like the one I wanted to paint the previous day.

I reach for one of the brushes, but something doesn't feel right. One of my spotter brushes is wet. I bring it to my nose and smell it—wet paint.

I don't remember painting the previous night.

In the corner of the room are stacks of canvas I don't recognize. I walk towards them.

I pick a piece from the stack. I can't see well, but from the strokes, I see it's a painting of narrow leaves, long tubed shapes with petals and flowers. I can hear Luke's footsteps; he is coming toward the room.

The doorknob turns, and the door swings open. He says, "Why are you awake so early?"

I shrug my shoulders and stare at my husband. He smiles.

"Let's get back in bed; it's a few more hours before morning."

I pretend to look away, back at the piece I don't remember painting. It feels wet.

Please say something. I need to take the mask off your face. I know you are a lying bastard and a cheater, but this camouflage is killing me. You are a chameleon, a puzzle I can't seem to solve. My life is, anyway.

Luke says nothing. Not about the painting, nor anything else, yet he is waiting.

I should say something. Should I ask him about the painting? No.

I stand up and place the piece along with the others. I walk towards him.

In bed, I lay there and think.

I feel frustration gush through me.

I hate myself; she is void.

The worst feeling is seeing myself in pain, yet I'm helpless.

I cry.

I slowly fall into a dream, or should I say nightmare?

I can hear my heart thump loudly. My foot is caught in a tree trunk. A snap sound echoes into the night. My body is falling, I'm tumbling down, my skin hits against a pile of earth, and I can feel its clay taste on my tongue.

I brush myself off, and my hand sweeps over my elbow. It has a wet-dry leaf stuck over it. I'm running down a wooded area, but why?

There is a bright light; brimming from a distance, seemingly from a torch light. For some reason, I don't think the light is here to rescue me. Still running. Someone, a figure, is calling my name, no, two figures. A man and a woman.

"Klair..."

I open my eyes to see Luke. His tall figure gives me this heart-quivering feeling. The way he calls my name, its resonance, is like the voice in my nightmare. My skin is dripping from sweat. He is staring at me.

"Are you okay? Did you have a nightmare?"

Why is he asking? What should I say to this man? I nod my head to his question. He can take it any way he wants to. I stand up and head toward the bathroom. My nightgown feels damp from the rain in the nightmare.

Luke is knocking on the bathroom door. I hate this man; the pretense that he cares when he wants me dead is repulsing. Does he want to kill me? Every time his shadow looms outside the door, I feel a shriek escape my mouth, though I try to replace it with soft tunes of lullaby; it helps. Am I just living in my head?

"I will be right there," I say.

I open the door, and he hands me a cup of tea. The Jasmine tea, I presume, the one that has a bitter and stale aftertaste.

I stare at him, then take a sip off my cup. My hands are shaking, but I need to be calm. I can't let him see my fear. I bring the cup to my lips and pretend to sip. Luke stands up.

"I'm heading to bed."

I pretend to sip again, then promise to join him in a minute. I stare into the space of the living room. I must speak to Ryan again; he can help me unravel this mystery interlocked into my memory. I walk towards the kitchen sink and pour down the tea.

Chapter Ten

Klair
I take a deep breath and listen to the guest ramble down the hall about her painting. She had ordered Teri Hook's *Dearest*, acrylic on canvas with abstract style, two-dimensional lines, and strokes. However, she received Kristin Lloyd's *My dear*, oil on canvas with linear style and subtle brushstrokes.

Cindy is down the hall talking to the guest, who is very angry about the mistake.

I have been studying most nights on art, exhibitions, and even artists. Yes, I have color blindness, but I can tell some parts apart. These are two different paintings in style and brush strokes. The strokes and individual application to artwork are like a fingerprint. They distinguish every artist from another, but how did I make this mistake? Probably because of having those flashes at the moment when these art pieces were being wrapped to be sent to the guest who had bought them.

I can remember that moment. It wasn't my mind playing tricks with me again. I saw myself through what seemed like broken mirrors: Pieces of my life played in front of my eyes: I was seated at a restaurant. I could tell because beside me sat two couples with a menu. They spoke in a soft tone. In front of them was a waiter who continuously gestured to the menu the couple was reading. From therestaurant's door walked in an older woman who placed her walking stick beside her chair. Then, a woman of average build walked in. She approached me with something in her hand. What was it?

In an airy voice, she said, "Hi, Klair Knox. I appreciate your meeting me. My name is Deby Williams."

I remember that I reached my hand towards her for a handshake when the flashes went away, and the art was already packed for delivery.

Now

I stare at the museum floor; it feels rubbery. I rub my hand over the pleated skirt I am wearing. I glance over. Cindy and the guest are still talking. Someone is tapping my shoulder. I can feel chills run down my hand. I turn around, and it's Ryan. This man startles me often, always tapping me on the shoulder.

"Hey, Klair," he says.

I know he must have heard about the mistake I made, so I say, "I'm sorry, Ryan, for the mess."

He pats my shoulder.

"It's okay, Klair; mistakes happen. I believe Cindy can sort this out."

I stare at him and feel grateful and conflicted about what I'm about to say. "Hey, Ryan, can I have a favor?"

"Okay, Klair." He rests his hand over the wall.

I scratch my head like it holds the words I'm about to say. "Do you know anyone who can help me find someone?"

"Who are you looking for?" he asks.

"My mum. I have asked Luke about her, but he is very evasive, but I believe she might have answers for me."

"Let's talk in my office, Klair; we don't want to distract the guests."

He walks toward Sonia and whispers something to her. What did he say to her?

He turns towards me, and we begin to walk towards his office. I say, "I also had a flashback of me meeting Deby."

His eyes widen as he opens the door to his office. "You did?"

I take a seat with my hand placed over the oval-shaped glass table in Ryan's office. It has stacks of files, and for a second, I feel guilty for adding my problem to his. He is already a busy man, yet he is willing to help. Come to think of it, how did he know I was with Luke? Does he know about Dr. Mallot, too?

"Luke is my boss, not my friend, Klair. You can talk to me, it's okay," he says with a smile.

Can he read minds? Can I trust him?

"Do you remember anything about your mum before the memory loss?" he adds.

"I know she was institutionalized, but I can't seem to recall the name of the place."

"Have you tried to search your home? Luke could have left some receipts or anything linking to her whereabouts around the house."

I have thought of that before, but with the way Luke cleans the house and has most of the desk drawers locked, I believed searching the house would come to nothing, which is why I followed him the other day to the hospital.

"No," I reply.

"Search the house, Klair. Do you think Luke is lying to you?" He places his hand on the table too.

"I don't know what to believe, Ryan." I run my eye for a lamp stand next to the wall. "He is always evasive about everything: my mum, his family, the memory loss, and even the accident."

"Do you live on 1631 West Oak?" Ryan begins to type something into his computer.

"Yeah. Why?"

"Nothing..." He looks at the printer, which is now whirring. "Just asking. I have a friend who works in the Calitain special unit. I will ask for his help on your mum's case."

"Thank you, Ryan."

"You seemed shaken some minutes ago on the exhibit floor. Do you want to go home for the day?"

I really would love to go home, but if I were to take such a special privilege when others are still here at ten a.m. in the morning, I will attract more hatred. I shake my head. "No, I'm good, Ryan."

Chapter Eleven

Klair

Earlier today, I spoke to Ryan, but it has left me with more questions than answers. In his words: "Klair, start finding answers on the things you know, then the things you don't know will come."

I jump into Luke's truck as we are about to go home; the repulsing smell from the previous night still lingers. I need to check the house when I return from work, but one thing is bothering me.

Luke, my sweet and loving husband, might not leave the house. Just thinking about it alone makes me gasp for air.

We pull in front of the house, and I open the door, but he rolls the glass window down.

"Klair, I'm hanging out with the guys."

Does he know what I'm up to? Is he onto me? It still feels suspicious, but I must take my chance rather than not do anything. According to Ryan, I have been doing just that for eight months—nothing.

My stomach churns with butterflies. My feet feel like they are floating in thin air while I watch him drive away.

He would be back in an hour, I believe. All I need is ten minutes. I get into the house, immediately shutting the door behind me. First, I check our bedroom where, of course, I don't find anything, and then I go to my studio.

I don't bother to check the other room, which is empty. Like a curious cat, I begin to dig around my studio, around the area with the wet canvases, which, of course, I'm not surprised are not there anymore.

Nothing startles me anymore when it comes to my life in this house, or so I think.

The room isn't difficult to search since it is a little studio-like room with a blank canvas on an easel and two painted canvases on the left; they've been there for as long as I can remember. On my right would have sat the wet canvases, now missing.

I almost give up my search until my foot feels a bump on the floorboards, making a creaking sound.

I run my hand over it to investigate. The floors feel uneven, so I reach for the ends of the carpet against the wall. I pull it towards me and what appears in front of me is an iron latch.

I pull up on it and find a staircase beneath it. I can feel a dry cough follow, then watery and itchy eyes. I turn on the flashlight from my phone and slowly walk down the stairs.

Every step I take comes with a creaking sound. A basement-like room with ceramic walls and rubber flooring opens up in the expanse at the bottom of the stairs.

A strong, sweet, and tangy smell blows through me. It is the same smell Luke always has an evasive excuse for. I squint my eyes as I quickly look around the room. On the left floor sit the wet canvases. On the right is what I'm still staring at.

A dripping sound is making the space eerie. I stare at what is in front of me: the face of death. I can feel my palms become moist, my heart rhythm racing.

My eyes are so watery that I continue to cough. How did it come to this? To my finding a dead body hidden beneath the canvases?

I can't feel my legs, and my hands are shaking. I'm staring at what seems like nothing other than a dead woman's body. It is wrapped and leaning against the room's wall, and beside it is the faucet that is dripping water.

Pick-Sea, call 191: I say to the virtual assistant on my phone.

It's been a few minutes since I made the call. I still can't move, but I can hear footsteps above me. Is someone speaking?

"Klair Knox, that's the name of the caller?"

The bright light of a torchlight shines from the stairway. I bring my hand towards my face to cover my eyes from the harsh light. Someone is coming down into the room—no, three people. They are police officers, I think.

"Close this area down. We have a crime scene here!" one of the officers' voices echoes through the room. He is walking towards me.

"I'm Rex Dilaud. Can you tell me what happened?" he says.

I can feel my body growing cold; the hair around my neck have suddenly risen. He is asking me about how I found the body, but the words aren't coming out.

Where do I start? Me losing my memory? Me suspecting my husband? Or, do I lie about me just walking into a secret compartment in the home where I live with my husband and finding a dead body? Where do I start?

The light from the torches is bothering my nerves—I don't like them. Did someone turn on the AC all of a sudden? I stare at the short man with a trimmed beard and a holster on his side.

"Klair," another voice is calling me.

It's Luke, but I don't feel happy seeing that voice actor.

"Ma'am?" The annoying voice of the detective comes again. "You called 191 this evening, and I need to know the incident that led to..."

His words are cut short, and another voice echoes; she is coming down the stairs. "Rex," she says, with her hand gesturing to the officer who is in front of me.

The officer walks towards her. Behind her is Luke, but he isn't allowed to come down the stairs.

I can hear the officer speak distinctly to her. "I think she is pleading the fifth."

"Her identity has been verified; she is Klair Knox," she says.

There is chatter from the radio; she reaches to press the button and speaks. The officer who was in front of me is coming towards me again. "Klair Knox," he says, "we need you to come with us to the police station for a few questions."

But why? I wonder. I want to ask but don't. I see Luke. He is staring at me. I ask, "Am I under arrest?"

The officer turns around and stares at me. "Are you ready to give us your statement?"

My leg is trembling. I feel weak and I don't think I can walk any longer. I can feel my body grow numb. I'm falling, and the world is growing dark.

Chapter Twelve

K^{lair}

I play back to what little I got to know about my life after finding a dead body in a secret room under the house. Likewise, I remember Luke's words to the detective. "My wife had an accident last spring and doesn't remember anything at the moment."

He made me sound incompetent and helpless. Now, I know why he has kept me so close beside him, not filing for divorce, even though he has a mistress. It's like a daunting game to him, and he must be enjoying the thrill of it.

Also, there was a lawyer at the scene, the type my dad hired to relinquish custody of me. I know that Luke makes okay money, but how could he afford such an expensive lawyer, who with a few words to the detective, allowed Luke and I to just walk away?

I look around for Luke and realize he is driving—so unnerving like we didn't just find a dead body in our house. Like we weren't just interviewed by the police. He is just driving; I don't know where we are going. I run my eyes over the streetlights as they hurriedly pass by us. I feel a flush of hot air tower over me. I say, "Where are we going?"

"We can't stay at the house. It's a crime scene!" he says, but he isn't answering my question. Though the car is dark, I can see his hand pull into a tight fist. The veins under his skin so visible.

"Luke, where are we going?" I ask again.

"Home," he replies.

What is this man saying? The house is under investigation, he just said we can't stay there, but we are going home. "What home, Luke?"

He stops the car. I don't know why. What is he doing? He steps out of the car, and I take a few seconds to think.

He begins pacing outside the car.

"Klair, what do you want from me? Everything I've done has always been for your good." He kicks hard on the car's tire, then raises his hand in the air.

I step out and walk towards him. I don't seem to understand what he means. I look up and down the street. Some cars are honking at us as they go by.

Luke's car is parked on the side of the street. A restaurant and a beauty salon are next to us, but nothing looks familiar. I tuck both hands under my sweater; it's the only thing that seems familiar to me. I say, "What do you mean, Luke?"

He is still pacing. He walks towards the driver's door and slams it shut. "After you told me that your mum was missing, you insisted that we stay at her place in case she came back; that's what we have been doing, Klair, staying at your mum's."

My heart drops and a sudden urge to vomit comes over me. I still don't understand this man. "My mum has been missing? Since when?"

He walks away. "I don't know, Klair, but all I did was what you wanted—staying at your mum's," he repeats the words.

I don't have any memory of my past, but of the little I know, my mother was institutionalized. Why was my mum missing? Luke presses the car key, and a chirping sound echoes into the night. "What has my mum got to do with the house and the dead body?" I ask.

I'm not sure whether what he just told me is the truth. I ask, "How come you withheld so much from me, Luke? Information about myself, my mum, the house; how come I don't know anything?" I place my hand on my waist and shake my feet. This reminds me of Angel Betty from hell. She must have felt this way all those times she tormented me.

"I don't know, Klair, maybe because I was working too hard to protect you," he says.

"Protect me from what, Luke?"

He walks away. "Get in the car, Klair."

I cross my arms over my chest. "You know what, Luke?" I begin. "I need answers, and I'm not getting into that car until I get some."

Lies, all he says are lies. His mouth opens, and lies fall out. I think of the nurse at the hospital. She addressed him by the name *Mallot*. I want to see how he will lie his way out of this.

"So, Luke..." I begin. "Is your last name Mallot? And, when were you going to tell me about it?"

I look up to see Luke closing the door to the car. He turns on the ignition and drives away, leaving me standing there.

Am I surprised? I reach into my sweater pocket; I skim through my phone. It has only two numbers. I dial Ryan's.

Chapter Thirteen

Abbey Mallot

This evening, my phone rings, and I can hear my son speak with a trembling voice.

He says, "Mum... I made another mistake."

I wouldn't call it a mistake but a bad judgment. My son is a good boy. He is the best child one could ever ask for. He's a straight A's student with scholarships and a promising future, except for a one-time cloud of judgment where he beat his classmate to a pulp. The other child, as of now, wears a hearing aid due to damage to his eardrum.

It was the other child's fault. He provoked my son to do it out of jealousy. My poor son watched his father act out his anger on his mother while growing up. I blame that useless father of his for my son's mistake.

I have done what any mother would do to protect her child. Not only that, but I have done it several times and will keep doing it. Like when that college girl said my son raped her. That was a lie; all she wanted to do was destroy my son's future. I know she lied because she dropped the case after I paid that wench twenty thousand dollars. She did it for the money.

Klair's mother makes me laugh through my teeth. That woman who left her daughter. That addict had the nerve to talk to me about my son; she called him a bad son. That dumb woman was always spewing nonsense from her lips. Whatever happened to her, she had it coming. And Klair, or is it, Clare? Sometimes I find it hard to tell who is who—that low-life who couldn't distinguish between an instant coffee and a civet.

My son dated someone who was out of his class, yet she turned around to pay him back with evil. She was going to send my only child to prison. That lucky witch survived that night.

What was Luke thinking, getting her a job at the museum? That girl, Clare, has only bad intentions when it comes to her being involved in his life.

My heart nearly dropped during the last session when she said she remembered. It was like I was in front of one of her paintings: a portrait of a murder scene.

I told him to divorce her, but my son wouldn't listen. He says keeping her close is a better idea. Well, I think my idea on that night was the best.

I called her about a therapy session this morning, but she was evasive over the phone. Does she know that I'm Luke's mum and I have been lying to her?

I will set up another one by tomorrow. This girl is an enigma, very difficult to figure out. The truth is she scares me.

I know I might lose my license for what I have done. I have a faulty therapist relationship with her, all because I want to know what she remembers. The truth must be contented, right? After all, revealing the truth to me about what she remembers about that night is better than telling someone else. No one else will understand why I did what I did. No one else will protect my son the way I always have. No one will protect him the way I always will.

My son is a good boy. This isn't a mantra or a wish. He is a good boy, and I will protect him.

Chapter Fourteen

K^{lair}

Klair

This morning, I walk into a restaurant. I sit next to the window and feel the morning rays against my skin. It feels good.

I look around the restaurant; it reminds me of the one in my flashback where I met Deby. I can feel my feet move slightly to the beat of the music playing in the background.

I stare out at the street, where everyone seems to be in a rush. The buzzing sound of cars and construction machines—this is what life outside of the fence I live behind with Luke feels like. Even with the chaos, I hear the beauty and feel at peace. This is real.

I feel a tap on my shoulder. I don't feel startled anymore because I know it's Ryan. I turn around towards him. "Hi."

He is my boss, but I decided I could be more comfortable with him after yesterday. After Luke dropped me off and drove away, I called Ryan, and he got me a hotel to stay in for the night. It has been two weeks already since I began working at the museum, and according to HR, I should be paid.

"What's today?" I ask.

"Wednesday, Klair. You know this is the third time you have asked me that; your payday is in two days." I watch him take a seat opposite me.

Ryan gestures to the waitress and drops his wallet on the table. A wallet should have a driver's license and bank cards in them. I make a mental note to find out if I have any of these. I'm glad I'm beginning to realize how much I don't know about myself. Though I hate accepting I relied on Luke for everything.

"What do you want for breakfast?" he asks.

I reach for the menu that sits on the table and scan through it.

"I want the All-dash egg omelet." I set the menu down confidently, pleased I could finally choose my own meal. My eye catches Ryan's, and he smiles.

"I made a call to a source of mine, and he says the…" The waitress arrives at that moment, and Ryan looks at her. "Two plates of the All-dash egg omelet," he says with a smile.

He sets the menu down as the waitress walks away. "According to my source, an autopsy is being performed at the moment." Ryan rests his hand on the table and rubs his thumb over his fourth finger. "They haven't identified the body yet, though my source says it's a female in her fifties."

The memory of the wrapped body flashes through my mind. I shake my head to clear the image. I can feel cold sweat run down my back.

I don't remember being close to my mum. I have no idea how old she was or would be at this moment, but for someone in her fifties, she would perhaps have an older daughter or son around my age.

"How did you live in the house if a decomposing body existed there? It must have smelled bad." Ryan's words pull me out of my deep thought. I remember the strong, sweet, tangy odor I often smelled, especially in the room I tried to paint in, and how bad it was on the days the AC wasn't working. I pick up the cutlery from the table, trying not to think about it; Luke lied about it being broken.

"It did, but I didn't know what it was," I reply.

"About your mum…" I watch him reach into the front pocket of his shirt and bring out a piece of paper. "She is at Mary Oaks Nursing Home on Cambridge Street."

My eyes widen. I drop the cutlery back on the table and reach for the paper. "Thank you, Ryan."

"Do you want me to come with you?" he asks.

"No. I want to do this by myself, Ryan," I say confidently. I have been left in the dark for too long, having to depend on others. Meeting my mum finally, I want to do it by myself.

"There is something that is bothering me, Klair," he says. The waitress arrives with our food; she places it on the table and walks away. "The address from Deby is different from what Luke has on his company profile."

I recall Luke's words the previous night: "I'm taking you home."

"Luke said the place we live in is my mum's, and we're staying there until she returns?"

"Until she returns?" he asks.

"He claims my mum is missing, but Ryan..." I look at the piece of paper he gave me. "It's best I visit the nursing home and see for myself."

I spoon the egg and bring it to my mouth, my eyes darting from wall to wall of the restaurant; the round-shaped counter reminds me of the flashback.

"Ryan, about Deby; I think I met her, and handed something like a canvas to her."

I watch him drop his fork on the plate. "I have it, Klair, but it has nothing on it; it's a plain canvas."

I wonder why I would have handed a plain canvas to Deby. I also think of the accident. What happened to Deby, and when? Was it after I gave her the canvas? Would what's in that canvas lead to her being in danger or me having an accident? What type of accident was it?

I watch Ryan take a sip of his drink. He seems to hold more answers than I do and isn't evasive like Luke.

"Ryan, do you know when the accident happened?"

"August 18 is the last time I spoke to Deby when she told me she was meeting you."

"Why was I meeting her?" I ask.

"Deby didn't tell me much, only that you were an informant on Luke's…" He takes a deep breath, his eyes staring at the omelet as if it holds the words.

Luke must be involved in something illegal, and I was going to be an informant. For a second, I can't help but smile to myself. I must have been brave before the memory loss.

"Is Luke involved in something that could cause harm to the museum?" I ask.

I watch Ryan shake his head in affirmation. "But we don't have the evidence, and you were going to provide it," he replies.

So, the canvas must be that evidence, but it's a plain canvas, something like my painting, strokes, and unfinished lines.

Chapter Fifteen

L uke
        I can feel my heart thump. These damn nerves are driving me crazy. Yesterday, I was angry. Yeah, I know, I'm always angry. My mum minces words. She says, "Luke, you are stressed, displeased, unhappy, and irritated."

Yeah, I'm all of the above, all the time. Don't they all mean I'm an angry man?

She just doesn't say it to my face. Klair had the nerve yesterday night. She wouldn't stop talking, so yeah. I stopped the car and left her there, but by the time I went back, she was gone. Does she know about mum? She mentioned my last name yesterday. I wasn't going to wait there and let her play detective.

Where could she have gone? I can feel my hands shake; I need to take a smoke. I wonder if she has come to work this morning.

Relax? How can I be relaxed when that memory of hers could come back with a snap of a finger. Unfortunately, I haven't been able to add the powdered herb mum asked me to add to her tea every evening.

I take a deep breath. That's what I should do. She could all of a sudden begin to paint a fucking crime scene or call the cops again—not for her mother's freaking corpse that I hid in the house, but for what I did to her throughout our marriage.

I need to find out what art pieces that stupid girl handed to Deby Williams. How long had she been putting together all this evidence? I should have known she was up to something when she pretended to be all nice and friendly, even when my mother hated her and was against my decision of marrying her.

I mean, she looked like a freaking angel, and I counted myself lucky for once. I nearly used lucky as my baptismal name. Lucky? I'm about to laugh through my teeth. I must have been that dumb to not know what she was planning.

I should take a deep breath and not try to think about it, though I'm about to punch a hole into this damn wall, but then, it's a glass wall. My office is furnished with expensive modern furniture that I normally wouldn't be able to afford, not in a million years.

The house I bought for us came from that same money. That hypocrite hated the one-bedroom apartment we lived in before the new house I bought, yet she was going to act all righteous all of a sudden. When I met her, she was just some poor painter on the street earning dimes; and I was a university student studying business management. We worked hard together and began to build a life, then one day she grew a conscience... Fuck her.

Even more, she was going to turn everything over to the police. That bitch is very vindictive. It's like she takes it all, but when she bounces back, she hits you right in the head, and trust me, it's going to hurt.

I tried to get the artifact from the police, but they refused—something about holding onto it for an investigation.

Someone is knocking on my door. Who is it? Oh, it's her. The woman in my life who has made me begin to think of being better. But why does she have a wig on?

"What's wrong with your hair?" I ask.

She closes the door and walks towards me. "Why? Do I remind you of Klair when I have my hair short?" she asks.

She shouldn't ask that; she is intelligent, beautiful, and everything I could ever ask for.

"Is she at work?" I ask.

"Are you worried about her? I think I saw her walk into Ryan's office this morning. Those two must be up to something." She walks closer, and I detect her intoxicating smell of Jasmine—I love it. "Why do you ask about Klair? You are making me jealous."

Her voice. So sexy. I can't find words to describe her, but she is perfect.

"When did your words become so bitter and twisted?" I ask.

She scoffs and looks away. "I just can't stand that she works with you, and I have to steal your attention from another woman." She pulls away and walks towards the door, is she kidding? Staying married to Klair is just because... Well, I don't want to go to prison, though I feel safe now. With the memory loss, I mean.

And speaking of Ryan, didn't that fool mention he doesn't have Klair's painting with the anagram KK? I thought he got Deby's property from the police after the accident. It's been eight months since the accident, and I have been calling for an update on the investigation.

After hearing the same story repeatedly about the artifact being held for an investigation, I might have stopped calling about it, but I became indifferent.

I don't surprise myself. That's how I am. At times, the passion in me burns like fire and brimstone, and the next moment, I become lukewarm with nothing to motivate me.

I was that way on the night of the accident. After I learned that Klair had handed the pieces to the police, I said to myself, *Well, let fate have its own damn way and do whatever it wants.* When mum found out that Deby had the evidence, she wasn't having it.

That's mum; she has always protected me and Dad, though that dirtbag left us for his political career. She always went way and above to protect us.

Last night, I called the unit overseeing the investigation and was told someone had signed for it. If it wasn't Ryan, who has it? I must speak to him soon about it. The data she encrypted into her painting must be on that piece.

She should have just stayed quiet and minded her own damn business. I was stealing money from the museum, not from her. Yet, she thought she had to create a freaking ledger, which she hid in a painting; such incriminating evidence would send me to prison.

"I don't want to be the mistress, Luke," she says.

"You know why I'm with her. Come on," I say. I walk towards her, and she purses her lips. I don't like that.

She is wiping her eyes; is she crying? I stare into her eyes. "Lily, you asked me the secret to the painting," I call her by the name she prefers rather than her real name.

Her head nods up and down. "What about it? Because I have been brushing off her already painted canvases and repainting them, but I just can't find a clue as to what she is hiding."

I want to tell her the secret, but I'm holding off. This secret involves a lot of people. This is bigger than her paycheck and mine, and these people aren't going to prison because a little girl went around being nosy. I can see a crisp line run across her forehead. "Patience—that's what you asked me to have. Two years is a long time, Luke," she says.

Chapter Sixteen

K lair

I walk into a large hall with dim lighting. The attendant, a young lady with short hair, sits behind the desk.

"How may I help you, madam?"

"I'm here to visit my mum," I say.

She hands me a clipboard; it has a COVID questionnaire attached to it. "Please go ahead and fill that out for me."

I take a seat, ticking off the 'no' sections of the questionnaire. I can feel my hands are damp, and my heart thumps loudly. I can't wait to meet my mum, though I can't remember much about her. I know our relationship wasn't that great.

Mum couldn't keep a job, and Dad wasn't supporting us financially. With their shiny black suits, the lawyers who made money every time they said a word helped Dad relinquish legal custody of me. In Mum's words: 'That idiot says you aren't his daughter. He would rather the child his wife adopted be his daughter.' Even a DNA result was said to have been forged by Mum to provide evidence that I was his child, though he constantly referred to me as a bastard.

And from there, it never got better. Mum drowned herself in alcohol, taking solace from the illusion it provided. She got ill after a while and had to be hospitalized. This caused my relationship with her to become strained.

I remember visiting her occasionally in the company of Mrs. Betty or a social worker. Angel Betty from Hell, the evil angel who made me work without meals in my stomach. She found reasons to yell at me, finding satisfaction in my tears. It became worse when I spoke out to the social workers.

I turn my focus back to the hall, trying to sense the familiarity with the one I had visited, just in case I'm at the wrong place. I remember on one of my visits, I cried and asked mum to get better and take custody of me, but her health only worsened.

I raise my head from the form, and the attendant smiles at me. Walking into one of the halls, I see the shape of someone familiar with a short bob hairstyle, but it might just be my imagination.

A line on the form reads: *What is your relationship to the person you are visiting?* I proudly write: daughter. I walk towards the attendant, who pages someone over the phone, and soon a tall, plump-looking man approaches me.

"Hi," he begins.

I should be allowed to see my mum, but this man meets me instead. I notice his uniform and the badge that reads: Andrew Stranc Admissions Nurse.

"Are you Klair Knox?"

"Yes," I nod my head in affirmation.

"It says you are Mrs. Lair Cruz's daughter, and you are here to visit her?"

I smile, rubbing my palms over one another. "So, can I see my mum?"

He coaxes his brow, then says, "Follow me." I walk into a small room with a cabinet and a green folder, which has numbers on it. On his desk are other folders containing forms with the words: Discharge Instructions. He closes the folders and pushes them aside.

"Take a seat, please."

I take a seat, and I realize my throat is dry. I watch him type something into the computer, and then he looks toward me.

"Mrs. Knox, your mum was discharged two years ago." He clicks on the mouse pointer and turns the screen towards me. "You discharged your mum."

"I did what?" I say, my throat even more parched, the words barely there. He clicks the next screen.

"Here is your signature and scanned driver's license. Your mum was discharged to your care." My driver's license. I don't remember ever having one or driving. Luke. I bite my lip at that name. I have been a fool to believe him all these months, or for however long this has been going on.

"She was discharged at two fourteen p.m. on the sixteenth of July 2020." He continues, pointing at the screen, "What's going on?"

Andrew raises an eyebrow, and my mind like a maze. He wants to call the director of nursing but I leave.

I walk out of Mary Oaks Nursing Home with more questions. I can't help but feel a chuckle escape my lips. I discharged my mum, who I came to visit—all jokes on me due to memory loss. I can feel warm air escape my lungs as I laugh.

"Madam, you forgot your purse." I turn around, and it's the receptionist. She hands over my purse and runs back inside.

The cold air coming from the hall as she runs back in swiftly touches my skin. I rub my bare shoulder with my sweaty palm. I can feel cold sweat across my back, and my throat tightens.

Oblivion isn't a blessing but a curse. The doctor said that what I had forgotten was protecting my body from something.

I lived in a home with a dead body, with a man who lies to my face; I see a therapist who, every time I'm about to ask a question, I can see her lips quiver.

The admissions nurse said I used my driver's license to discharge her. I will have to get a replacement for my driver's license, now that I know I used to drive. I bring my phone out to dial, but who? I should go to the police station to report her missing. Sure, Luke mentioned that my mum is missing, but I don't trust a word he says. Was he telling the truth? Should I call him? Will he tell me more rather than being evasive? I sigh. I don't trust him; he said we filed a missing persons' report, but the truth is, the police might not even know that my mum is missing.

The sound of a car horn breaks me out of thought. I don't think I have seen this car before. I bend down and take a peep at the driver, who winds down the car's window. I gasp.

"Sonia, what are you doing here?"

"Girl, I bet a thousand bucks that was you. I came here to visit my granny."

"Wow," I say, though I question the sheer coincidence of meeting Sonia in a different part of town away from the museum with a million words.

"Aren't you supposed to be at work?" I ask.

"Makes the two of us!" She runs her finger over her steering wheel, then lets out a loud laugh. "Need a ride? Hop in."

With my phone still on the contact list screen, I dial Ryan's number as I step into the car.

"Going anywhere special?" She blows a bubble with her gum, then continues to snack on it like it holds the question and isn't asking me why I'm here. Anyway, it's best because I can't tell her I'm about to go to the police department to file a missing persons' report for my mum.

"Do you live around here?" I abruptly ask.

"Yeah." Sonia turns on the ignition, and we drive through a bumpy road with trees, which seems like a swarm.

I took a taxi here, so might not have noticed this road on my way here.

"You live far from work," I say, my eyes glancing at her car, which has leather seats and accessories. "Your car is cool too," I add.

"Thanks," she says. She reaches toward her head and pulls off her hair. "I love it when I'm off work; I can take this off."

"That's a wig?" I can see a resemblance to the short hair I thought I had seen walk down the hall of the nursing home.

"I hope you can keep my secret. I have a genetic disease, and alopecia is one of the effects," she says.

"It's okay, Sonia, your secret is safe with me. I might not even remember it tomorrow," I joke.

The car comes to a stop, and in front of us is a railroad crossing. The clicking sound of the train roars into the distance, and I look around; the vast land around us seems familiar. The smell of earth and Jasmine fills my senses. I have been here before.

"I hope you don't mind, Klair," Sonia begins, "I need to stop by my place before going back to work."

We arrive at a two-story building, and around it is a tall tree with twisted branches and narrow leaves. The high-pitched sounds of chirping birds can be heard in the distance, followed by cricket sounds. I glance at my wristwatch, and it's one p.m. already; the museum closes at six p.m. I follow her up the stairs of the building.

"Come in," Sonia says, reaching into a flowered vest sitting in front of her door and bringing out a key. I can feel my palms begin to sweat again. I bring my phone with me and text Ryan: *At Sonia's. Met her at the nursing home.*

I take a seat and watch Sonia pour me a cup of tea.

"Make yourself at home," she says. People around here, it seems, love their tea, though I can't recall ever loving or hating it. It takes a while for me to sip my tea. I still don't know Sonia—or what is in my cup.

"So, do you like your job at the museum?" she asks.

"Yes," I say as I look around the house—more spacious and brighter than I expected. A light, flowery curtain dances from one end of the window to the other. The carpet under my feet feels very soft.

A strong organic and chemical smell fills the air. I can't help but ponder about her. As an intern at a gallery, Sonia must make a lot of money to afford such a place.

My eyes spot a painting that pulls my attention—a familiar painting of narrow leaves, long tubed shapes with petals and flowers, the one with the wet paint. Sonia has been to my house! Is she the woman Luke met at the train?

Chapter Seventeen

K lair

A whistling sound pulls me away from the painting. Sonia asks, "So, what do you love about it?"

A distant drip sound follows her words, and she has a cup in front of her. She pours hot water from a kettle into it. "You know, the thing I find rude is when people give me a short answer to an open-ended question."

She fills the kettle with water from the tap and places it on the stove. I realize her tone is calm yet bitter. I must have been a little distracted admiring and wondering about her home since it's a new place for me.

"I wasn't trying to ignore you," I say. The thing is, I know very little about her, so I have no idea what or how much to say. Yes, Ryan said she knows more, but I'm still wary of strangers. Moreover, my instinct screams Sonia is the other woman. I stick with a lie. "I was just a little distracted."

"Distracted by what?" she asks, setting down her cup of tea in front of me, then taking a seat opposite me at the large dining table with six chairs. She must have a big family, I ponder.

"Nothing."

I bring my cup towards my lips. Sonia stands up and heads towards a vintage music player. On top of it sits what appears to be a video disc.

"Do people still play these?" I ask. Sonia reaches for a disc, which she places on top of a turntable. Music begins to play. She turns around and walks toward me.

"Stop playing coy with me. I know you remember."

"Remember? What exactly do I remember?" I ask, bringing my hand towards my temple. The music is too loud; my head hurts. I scream, "Please make it stop!"

She brings herself towards me, kneels in front of me, and says, "You can make this easier for us, or..." She stands up and lets the last word hang in the air.

My attention is diverted to the window, where the evening breeze forcefully blows against the curtains. The sun outside is so far from its horizon, yet it blazes like wildfire. "Anyway, I will still get the truth, Klair, by the time I'm done with you," she continues.

What does she mean by the truth? Why is she doing this to me? My head is throbbing. I scream, "Make it stop!"

I can hear her giggle, then the whistling sound of the kettle over the stove. She says, "A lot of people are unhappy, Klair, and when I say a lot, I mean a whole lot of people. Where is the freaking ledger?"

What ledger is she talking about? Why is she doing this to me? *A shrill cry from the kettle on the stove breaks my thought.*

"I thought it would be hidden at your mum's house or within these dull paintings of yours, but..."

"The wet painting was you?" The high pitch of the boiling water is so loud, "You and Luke" I can't bring myself to complete the words, my mouth feels dry.

A slamming sound pulls my attention towards the hot kettle, tumbling its way towards the wall. I can feel my body quiver. I can also feel a splash of hot water over my skin—it burns so badly. Why is she doing this to me? Why am I just sitting here and taking everything she throws at me? It feels like I can't move my body; it must be from the tea.

She takes a deep breath and then laughs again, this time with a cackle in her voice. "I had no idea cleaning a house takes so much energy. That's Nin com; your husband wasn't as stupid as I thought."

I hear a clicking sound. I glance toward Sonia. and she is putting on a heel. "Luke, that husband of yours, can bring out your sanity. All I did was clean that damn place of yours for him while he went to his office and sent his wife to the therapist's office."

She walks towards me, her body towering over me. For some reason I can't move; her voice is ghoulish, like the character from one of those Halloween movies. "Yet I found nothing: no flash drive or hard copy notebook with the ledger information. Where did you hide it?" Sonia laughs. "How about we do it this way?" She waves her hand into the air, mimicking an orchestra's conductor: an upward motion of her right hand. "I will give you answers to questions you have been asking, and in turn, you will give me the answers I need."

She gestures with her head bowed like I'm a crowd watching a final act unveil. Her right leg tips behind her. "I think this is a fair deal."

She sits in front of me, but I look away toward her balcony, where I see a banana peel.

"And just in case you are wondering why I'm doing this to you, it is definitely not a coincidence. If you are wondering why an innocent person like you is going through this, you are far from innocent. This whole thing began because of you... but where do I start?"

Chapter Eighteen

Klair

"Have you heard of Dablo?" Sonia asks as if I know the answer. "It's a contract group, like mercenaries, except we don't work with guns. Neither are we soldiers; we like to think of ourselves as the middlemen. We retrieve a product, get paid, and the transaction is over," she continues.

My eyes, glancing to her patio once again, see the banana peel. I try to bend down, but the pain is unbearable.

"Anyway, what are you most interested in?" She snaps her finger. "I know. Your mum."

She sets her drink on the table and begins to walk away. "Luke said you might look like you aren't close to her but..." she pauses, then sighs, "I have a lot of cleaning to do in my room."

The clanking sounds of her heel disappear into the space. I can finally move, though I still feel a little weak and dizzy. I reach into my bag. I had no idea these prescription drugs from Dr. Mallot would be helpful. With the investigation, I didn't have much time to unpack, so I carried it with me. I bring out two tablets, which I carefully drop into Sonia's tea.

I can hear her voice become louder the closer she gets to the living room. "Luke said she would prove useful if held as a hostage to threaten you from doing anything stupid, so all I had to do was use your driver's license, forge your signature, and discharge your mum."

She tosses a wallet on the table. "That's yours, and to answer your question, yes, the body you found in your home is your mum's."

A hard lump forms in my throat. My heart pounds harder as I launch towards her; my weak hand barely clutches her neck. "What did you do to my mum?"

Sonia laughs. "All you had to do was stay out of it. Why were you so concerned about the embezzled funds? What was it to you, Klair? Revenge?"

"What do you mean by embezzled funds?" I ask. My fingernails dig deep into her skin, but she doesn't flinch. It's like she doesn't feel pain, or perhaps I'm too weak from the drug.

"Kultant needed funds for his political campaign," she says.

I think about the name, and the senate elect on the TV visiting the presidential house comes to mind. "What has the senate elect got to do with this?"

I can feel her hand over my elbow. "Klair, are you acting coy, or are you just clueless?" Her hand grasps me hard, and she pulls me away. "You want to tell me that you don't know about Luke's relationship with his dad?" She pushes me away, and for someone with such a small frame, I can feel my body thud hard against the floor.

"Anyway," she reaches for the drink on the table. "You knew that Luke was siphoning funds from the museum which, like slush funds, were used for his father's campaign." She takes a sip of her drink. "So, you created a ledger with information of the stolen funds, dates, and transfers, and were going to take that to the authorities."

"So, because of all that, you killed my mum?" I ask, trying to get up from the floor.

"Don't get it twisted, Klair. That would be personal. As I said, I'm only a middleman; I don't do it personally. Ask Luke about what happened to your mum." Sonia sets her cup on the table.

"If it's not personal, why are you doing this to me?" I ask.

"Because if I can't find the ledger, and if Kultant doesn't have it..." she bends towards me, "Klair, I don't get paid. So, Klair, where is it?" She stands up and lets out a cackle. "You overstepped yourself, going after someone of such power and authority."

I can feel the dulling pain return. A cricket and the clanking sound of the train echoes in the distance. The world turns black: a blur.

I wake up, not aware of where I am. Sonia is in front of me, but she is walking backwards, saying something. Her lips move between intervals. Her hand is swiftly thrown into mid-air like she is trying to avoid something being thrown at her.

Sonia isn't afraid of me, is she? I walk towards her. The clanking sound of her stilettos is more annoying. She steps over something, the banana peel. Her hands' clench like she is trying to hold on to something, then she shields her face away. From what? I rush towards her but watch her body fall; a thud sound follows, and a puddle of deep crimson forms around her head.

"Klair..." I hear a familiar voice from behind. I turn aroun, and it's Luke. The expression on his face is like one who has just seen a ghost. He says, "What did you do again?"

What did I do again? Behind him are two officers, and they approach me swiftly. A clicking sound of metal, its cold seeps through my skin, and my feet feel weak.

This must be about Sonia, but I didn't push her nor kill her. One of the officers says, "Klair, you are under arrest for the murder of Lair Cruz. You have the right to remain silent. Anything you say can and will be used against you in a court of law. You have the right to an attorney. If you cannot afford an attorney, one will be appointed for you."

I listen to one of the officers read me the Miranda rights. I look around me, and Ryan runs into the house.

"Are you okay, Klair?" His eyes stare at my handcuffed hands. "It's going to be okay," he says.

"But I didn't kill my mum," I say. I look around and find Luke behind me. "He did it." I gesture, but the officer pulls me away.

I feel cold run through me, and my body shivers. I try to move my hands, but it's like they aren't mine. We get to the car, and I see a reflection of myself through its glass window. Short black hair and hazel eyes. She is me, and I embrace her. She doesn't need to be saved. I smile as my mind takes me down memory lane, and I recall who I am.

The Shattered Line
(Book Two Except)
How it all, began

Chapter 1

K^{lair}

SLAMMING.

Yelling.

Crying.

The sound always carried through the thin walls of our home. Unfortunately for me, it meant I heard Mum's grief every single time. The same thing happened tonight, but it seemed louder somehow; something crashed to the floor as her angry sobs and yelling echoed off the walls of my bedroom.

She was at it again. I couldn't blame her. Her addiction turned her into an entirely different person. I got up from my bed, moving to the small window beside me to open it. The cold wind flowed right into the small room, breathing on my face. I took a deep breath in return, sucking in the chill till it filled my lungs. I didn't mind the sharp shivers it sent down my spine—it was comforting. I turned back and saw the light that shone through the beige-coloured curtain separating my bedroom from the living room, illuminating the grey walls and pink bedding.

About a month ago, I'd chosen this room when we first moved in. I didn't do much customising, probably because I was unsure if calling it mine just yet was okay. All I had as proof was the fact that the man with the signature on my birth certificate said it was. That didn't count for much, considering he walked back into our lives for a few years before waltzing right out of them again two years ago.

I sighed, braiding the ends of my wavy brown hair as I heard another glass clank. I left my room to check it out, though I already knew who it was. My mum was sprawled out on the white leather couch, her long, chestnut-blonde hair fanned over the armrest. I still wasn't used to seeing her like that—so defeated and out of it. I knew wanting our lives to be different was like an *Unfinished Line*. It held no meaning, no matter how it was drawn. No matter what was drawn on it or how I looked at it, tilted it, or focused it, it remained.

Plain. No context.

No progress.

It was an obscure stroke of a painter's brush drawn onto a canvas, but I still hoped it could somehow change. I put in the work as her caregiver despite being only fourteen. If her getting better meant always keeping my bedroom door open and my eyes peeled to watch over her every movement, I was okay with it.

"Idiot," she slurred drunkenly at the television for what felt like the hundredth time. She hurled her bottle feebly at the small screen, and I was relieved that her throw was utter garbage when she was inebriated. I didn't want to have to sweep up broken glass in the morning or worry about replacing the TV.

The beer bottle rolled over to me, and its hollow, rolling clink against the wooden floor let me know it was empty. Mum would never throw a full one anyway. A part of me wished she would. It would be a good sign—like she was trying. But then, if she did, it would only mean I had to run to the store at the intersection to get more. I read somewhere that helping another's bad habits meant that you were enabling them.

If that were true, then I couldn't have been the only guilty one. Frank—the fifty-year-old guy with the beer belly at the corner store—was also guilty. He always gave me the bottles without even batting an eye at a fourteen-year-old shopping for alcohol or the single mum who kept sending her back frequently to buy more. Even when he did, he just asked about Mum—not in a concerned way; you've been here too often, though. His tone was always laid-back and chipper. If he suspected what was going on, then he didn't care. Or maybe he was just plain oblivious to it. After all, to him, we could be the near-normal mother-daughter who did errands that sometimes-included trips to get more beer. Who was he to judge, anyway?

The social workers who came to check on us occasionally could never find out about it. They wouldn't get a chance to either; we knew how to cover our tracks. The floors stayed swept, the dishes sparkled in their neat little stacks in the cupboards, and the bottles were nowhere in sight. I always wished this was our norm, rather than only when the social workers were coming, but it felt like I was the only one colouring over a ***Shattered Line***.

She started to yell again, this time at a man with a charismatic smile who had just appeared on screen. I might not be the drunken one, but I wanted to yell, too. Seeing him so tall and confident, talking about political things I could care less about was angering.

No matter how many times she said it, even with the genuine heartbreak I could always hear in her voice, I could never fully believe that this smiling man was my father. It was not hard to understand my reasons, either. Though they were together, they never married, and he was barely present in our lives—he visited once in a while because of his job until he never returned two years ago.

He'd gotten married, but it wasn't to my mum. I was supposed to believe that my father was the proper, well-groomed man with the moustache and tailored suit, a former news anchor and now senator of Calitain. If I hadn't met him, I would have thought it was another one of her alcoholic delusions. The yelling soon subsided, and she started snickering. I looked at the screen and then at her to see what was so funny. After confirming that there was nothing funny to laugh about, I could conclude that she was right about where she would start seeing Jerry.

Due to her being co-morbid with alcohol addiction and the sorry state of her mental health, hallucinations were common with her after five bottles, particularly about some guy named Jerry. I got up immediately in response to get her medication. She had already refused them this morning, so I didn't trust leaving her without them for too long. "Mum," I called as gently as I could when I went back with the pills in my hand.

I handed them over to her, keeping my voice calm and non-threatening as I said, "It's time for your meds. "She pushed my hand away, making my stomach knot up. There were times when she took them with little resistance, but it was always so nerve-racking to try to coax her into taking them when she refused.

"I already took them, Klair," she muttered, her frail hand fiddling with the edge of the blanket covering her. She barely ate. She hardly participated in anything aside from cursing my father on the TV for leaving her. I sucked in a breath, trying again to say, "I know, Mum, but you need to take them. It's twice a day."

She looked down at my hand again, and it felt like she would reach out to take it, but she shook her head. "But Jerry is here. If I take them, I won't be able to see him again." That was the point, but I held my tongue from saying anything to set her off. Though I could hear a bit of my frustration bleed into my voice as I spoke, "Mum, seriously. It would be best if you took them. You can't just skip a day. It's not good for you." When I tried moving the cap closer to her, her hand moved up to smack it out of my hand. The cap flew away, along with the pills. Though she didn't hit my hand hard enough to hurt, frustrated tears spilt down my cheeks.

I wiped my eyes before going to search for the pills and bottle cap on the brown hardwood floor. "It's okay. It's okay," I whispered, mainly to myself. At least we had a home now, and we were together. We used to stay at an apartment 'til we were evicted because Mum didn't get better and couldn't hold down a job or pay her bills. Then, she went away to rehab, and I was sent into foster care at the age of twelve. It wasn't until a month ago that she got released, and she thanked my father for signing her out.

We sat with him and his lawyer in this living room as he told me this would be our new home. And with it was a large sum of money in an account with my name on it to foot any other expenses, like school. He had no intention of raising me; that was pretty clear from the money and the fact that he just let Mum out without even caring or knowing if she had fully recovered and was stable enough to care for me. At least she looked presentable before him, with her hair neatly pulled back in a bun and her floral dress ironed to remove any creases. Nobody liked how she looked right now.

She snickered again. At least she was harmless, even with the hallucinations, but it still scared me to think about what would happen if Jerry ever started suggesting anything dangerous.

Since the straightforward method didn't work, I decided to go for my backup. I was not particularly eager to use it as much, as I didn't want to imagine what would happen if she ever found out. I headed towards the adjoining kitchen, opening the large fridge Dad had stocked. I had no idea if it was out of guilt.

"What flavour of ice cream would you like?" I asked, turning to face her from the tiled countertop, which gave me a good view of her on the couch; she was too caught in whatever conversation she was having with Jerry. "Mum, what flavour would you like?" I repeated myself louder this time.

"Oh? Um, peach, please," she answered.

I brought the peach-flavoured cup and set it on the counter with a spoon and bowl. I knew her eyes were glued to the screen anyway, but it did not stop me from looking over at her as I crushed the pills and put them in the bowl, making sure to mix them thoroughly with the liquid parts of the dessert. I brought it over to her, and she covered her face shyly.

"I can't. I'll get fat."

"It will be fine, Mum. You'll look lovely either way. I'm sure Jerry would like it too."

That seemed to get her attention because she blushed hard, taking the bowl from me. I stayed around to make sure she finished the entire thing.

To make sure she didn't notice me, I paid attention to the TV instead, where my father was making a speech with his wife, the one I learned was the daughter of Calitain's state governor. When I first learned about him, I searched the internet to learn everything about him, from his wife, whom he preferred to show the world instead of my mum, to his pretty little campaign that earned him that spot as a senator.

During my stay in foster care, all I did was write to him, making sure to pen down my rage and resentment at being left in foster care and my mum spiralling into alcoholism while he lived his perfect little life. I'm pretty sure that was what inspired the house and cash. He couldn't have some kid running around baring it all to anyone who would care to listen. It showed in his demeanour; he didn't even spare me a glance while his assistant did all the talking.

When she finished her ice cream and a bit of time passed, I could see it took effect as she dozed off on the couch. I covered her up with the quilt she made on one of her better days when the pull of alcohol wasn't so strong. I could still remember that day and the hope that came to life in my chest—hope that this was how she would be, that she'd put me above the alcohol.

My eyes stung from the tears welling up inside them, but I didn't like to cry in the house. So, I returned to my room to get my headphones and MP3 player, a Christmas gift from Madeleine, the social worker in charge of my case. She hadn't been by here, since Mum's discharge, but I knew she would be so disappointed, which would only be trouble for my mum and me.

I put on my headphones as I chose a playlist from the many, one of the kids from the foster home helped me download.

We weren't allowed to keep phones and other communication devices because of our family backgrounds and the reasons most of us were there in foster care, but in a short word, 'they were keeping us safe.'

I felt the evening cold seep through my skin as I pushed the blue wooden door of the house. It was only when I was safely outside that the tears could finally fall, sliding down my cheeks as my heart felt like it would burst open. I couldn't be away from Mum for long, but I needed this walk. It was hard for me to function with all those pent-up emotions in me.

Walking down the gravel sidebar, I approached the shopping centre. I watched the stores lined up at the sides, busy with evening sales. Customers walked in and out, talking and browsing through the wares.

As I walked past the restaurants, the scent of crispy fries in hot vegetable oil made my mouth water, even though I'd eaten a pretty good dinner of oven-baked pizza. It was easy to whip up for dinner.

I watched them wistfully, wondering what it would be like to be a part of that—not having to make trips to the corner store, but going where I wanted to go, or just eating out with Mum at one of those fancy restaurants. I never considered going to those places; they looked rather expensive, and I was unsure if the senator would give me more money if I wasted it like that.

I crossed the street, feeling my chest ache as I tortured myself with images of what could've been. The street seemed to blur as I moved on. My fingers tapped over my tights, slowly grazing over the cotton as the lively beat of the music streaming through my headphones created a sense of solace within me.

I had found a happy place until, without my knowledge, I crossed the street without checking the streetlight. The bright light from vehicles coming down the street shone onto me. My body froze, and it felt like my feet were stuck to the tar until I felt warm hands around me, and I heard the screeching of Tyre and the sickening thud. Clattering—the headphone and MP3 fell toward the centre of the street.

Loud honking-most of the cars, with bright lights and blaring horns, drove towards the side of the road or left the scene.

"Are you okay?!" a male voice called me out of my deep daze. I was lying on the ground, feeling as though a bucket of ice water had drenched my body, and I was unable to process anything else.

I stared around blankly. The dark tar was cold against my skin. It was a busy street, and some drivers stepped out of their vehicles. A young boy was in front of me. I couldn't make out his face from the blood dripping down his face to pool on the asphalt. All the activity I had envied stopped, as I spotted the people rushing out to see what had happened.

"Are you okay?" the same man asked as he reached for me. I wasn't sure as I stared at the boy who had pushed me out of the way and taken my place. Knowing that the warm hand, I felt, had taken the impact of the cold asphalt for me.

Chapter 30

L air
    I rubbed my hands together as I peeked outside through my door. I tried to keep my breath steady while tapping my feet nervously on the ground. Kelly, my caregiver for the evening, told me in a peachy voice that my daughter was here to pick me up. I asked her where Klair was, and she pointed at a lady in a black jacket and short black hair who, if my daughter had dyed her hair black, might have looked like the lady, but she wasn't Klair.

I knew I had issues remembering things sometimes, but I knew she was not Klair.

I wished I had a phone. I could call my daughter and tell her that some imposter was there. I knew that if I said it out loud to these people, they would think I was crazy, so I just stood, clutching to the purple teddy Klair had gifted me while I watched them speak in whispers outside my room's door.

I wondered what they could be talking about and if my daughter knew what they were up to.

I took slow steps, went back into my room and plopped down on my bed, staring at the untouched food on the table. They served me gluten pizza again for dinner after I had told them several times that I couldn't eat it. They did not think my opinions were valid. I was just a crazy patient.

I sighed as I looked out through the window. It was dark already, and if Klair had to come for me, she definitely wouldn't have done it this late. Whoever that girl was had an ulterior motive; after all, my life was not so interesting, and as such, no random stranger ever came looking for me.

I walked back to the door and watched the nurse. I prayed silently that I was not in danger, and neither was my daughter, Klair. She had been nothing but good to me. I did not deserve such a beautiful child. Soon, my nurse approached my door and pulled it open, giving me her best smile.

"I'm so excited for you, lair. Your daughter is here to pick you up. You are finally discharged. "

"No!" I screamed and shook my head. "That lady is not my daughter, "The nurse stared at me, then back to the lady. She shook her head like she either didn't understand what I said or what I said made no sense.

"Don't look at me that way," I yelled. "I know my daughter."

She looked around nervously and gave the strange lady a nod, signalling her to begin packing my things.

"Don't touch my things, I'll do it myself," I said, taking the bag from her hand.

"Wear this." The nurse threw a leather sandal on the floor towards me. "I'll leave you to it. Be ready in 15 minutes, okay?" she added as she walked out of the room and stood with the lady in the hall, leaving me to my raging thoughts. Who was this lady, and what did she want from me?

I ran my eyes for the slippers, I had been wearing since my admission into the nursing home, and its rubber sole was worn off.

I grabbed the teddy bear she got for me and squeezed it tightly to my chest, shutting my eyes. If this lady eventually took me, then that meant my teddy bear would not have been safe anymore, and I cherish it so much because it was the one thing that kept me close to Klair despite our distance.

The only way I could protect it was to hide it, so I got up and opened the window. A breeze of wind blew through it as a water drip touched my skin. I never knew it had been raining. I searched under the window for an old chair in the garden, where nobody sat. No one ever visited the garden.

Its flowers and once green grass were now brown with fallen decay leaves, which gave my room a strong muddy smell with an undertone of dew. I threw the teddy under the chair and checked to see if it had landed safely, and sure enough, it fell between its legs. I wiped the drizzled rain over my gown as I closed the window immediately to avoid drawing attention to myself.

Then, the door drew open, and the sound of its wooden frame against the iron frame made a grinding sound as the strange lady walked in. She flashed me a toothy smile:

"Hi, lair," she said in a very low tone but loud enough for me to hear. "or should I say hi, mum?"

I shook my head nervously.

She chuckled in response. "I'm not going to hurt you. It's me, Klair," she said, jabbing her index finger on her chest.

"You're not my daughter," I quickly interjected, but she only rolled her eyes at me as she picked my bag from the bed and urged me to follow her.

I watched silently as I was being signed out and taken out by this lady. The admission lady received a few slips of dollars from the nurse, hence only nodded to my discharge.

Minutes later, I was in the car as she drove off. It was a silent one until she parked at a parking lot. "Get some rest. We're going to your house in the morning," she said. I quietly sank into the seat, and my nerves raged until I slowly fell asleep.

THE NEXT MORNING, I woke up to an engine revving and realised that we were on the way home. Within minutes, we arrived at the roadside behind the house. A crowd gathered around someone who I believed was in an accident. I looked around, and my eyes caught my daughter. She was on her knees, her now short and black hair fell over her face which was burrowed into her arms. I slapped the car's window. "Wait" I looked toward her. "That's my daughter,"

The lady threw me a look, then back to her steering wheel as she continued to drive

"Stop," I said again, gesturing to Klair. "She is in some trouble."

Soon, we were at my single-family house. The lady was young, but her strong grip was one I couldn't wiggle free from. We climbed up the wooden steps. I stumbled as she pushed me towards the door; a thud sound cut my attention as I ran my eyes towards my right, and on it was Klair, who was dragged by Luke, similar to the way the lady did to me. Klair didn't seem to be alert.

"What did you do to her?" I glared at him. "Leave her alone."

Luke gave me a smirk as he dragged Klair onto the sofa, her head down like she was sleeping or perhaps dead.

"Is she okay?" I asked, but Luke walked away as the lady now stood behind me. My daughter was held in a hostage position, and I still did not understand what was going on.

"You just had to make a mess," I heard Abbey yell as she entered the room. That woman was still the same, always angry and hot-tempered. I still remember a faint memory from the past: I confided in her as my best friend while we were in college. I told her I liked a political science student named Jerry Kultant Mallot. She didn't know who he was before I confessed to her, but after that, my best friend announced to me the next day that she had met the love of her life and it had to be the same man. She had always wanted everything that was mine. Wanted to be like me, whom my parent, the Cruz, owned the best beer chains in Calitain, but that was before the bankruptcy and their death.

"Hi, Lair," Kultant said to me as he followed behind her. "It's been a long time," He added with a smile that looked like a wild animal's growl.

I glared at him. I had nothing on my lips, and he wasn't worth my words. He wasn't better than his wife. They both deserved one another. I remembered his crying when I told him I was pregnant for Knox, as I told him I was ending the entanglement of being his mistress. It was best he married his girlfriend, and though I loved him first, it was for everyone's happiness.

I still remember his scorn when I left him. He tried to destroy Knox's career as a news anchor. I had to go back to him to plead on behalf of Klair's father that he didn't harm his career. An affair that blossomed again, and Knox left me when he found out the truth. Kultant was the worst of them all, yet I loved the man who placed his own desires before others. I gave my heart and body to someone so vile.

"She was just going to turn that over to the police," Abbey yelled, not looking at me but at Klair. I looked down at my sandal, and the steel from its buckle, which had been bothering me, had pierced my skin. I unbuckled and took out my shoes as Kultant continued in a loud voice.

"So what do we do about my election?" He walked away from me towards Abbey. "If the press gets a hold of that canvas, it will be bad."

"The police should have her artefact, and I can get these" Luke said

"What will you use as an excuse to get closer to her items?" his mum asked

"She is my employee" He replied

I ran my eyes again for Klair, her head still bellowed, as I wondered if she was okay.

A few minutes later, Klair opened her eyes and scanned the room. I exhaled a breath I had not realised I was holding.

Her eyes settled on me, and I saw the battles she'd been fighting through her disturbed expression. She grew up fast, even though she was just a child. For the next few minutes, Abbey and Kultant yelled at my daughter about some evidence of a crime, which I had no idea about. Whatever this was, it must have been, the reason we were all there.

I recalled the purple teddy Klair had gifted me and a silver USB I found one day when I unzipped the back of the talking teddy. Could that have been the evidence they were talking about?

I was such a bad mother and did not deserve Klair. My past entanglement with this man put my daughter in this position, and I could not help her. I looked at her, and without words, I saw how her lips quivered, though the room was warm. The way her fingers shook. My Klair was scared, and this was all because of me.

A sudden blare from a siren from a distance caused the trio to be quiet. I turned towards Klair and mounted the words, "Klair, it's going to be okay."

The trio walked towards the window. The siren must have startled them. It could have been an emergency vehicle or a police call to a neighbour, but that was what happened when you did something bad-you lived in fear.

I suddenly remembered an emergency exit in one of the spare rooms. I found it one day in the house while cleaning, and it was on one of these days that I was clear-headed. I had taken a strolled out of it, which led into preservation de l'habitat, a forest behind my house.

I knew I couldn't spare a minute without giving it much thought. I had to save my daughter. She threw me a look, and like she knew what I was about to do, we stood up simultaneously, and she followed me. The room looked different, and it now had canvasses. Klair must have been painting there while I was away.

A smile of victory danced on my face as I continued to lead the way, running as fast as my legs could carry. I had always been a terrible mother who had never done anything for her daughter. This was the least I could do.

Outside, the wet soil burrowed into my bare feet. I turned towards Klair to see if she was following me. Her loud approaching steps as she jumped over a tree scrub gave me joy.

I turned around to continue running, and a splash of water over my leg came from a pool of muddy water. I could see that the forest was getting dark without my knowing. I struck my foot against a tree stump. It drove pain through my whole body, but that meant nothing. I turned again towards Klair, and this time, a figure was behind us, trying to catch up with Klair and me.

"Hurry," I said as I gestured to her, and then I slipped as my body found its way against a tree trunk. From a distance, I saw Luke behind Klair as he had finally caught up. I couldn't let the pain or the fall keep me down. I needed to save Klair.

I had no idea what had happened to me, but I rushed towards him like a mama bear filled with adrenaline. His back was behind me. He was dragging Klair down the stood-like hill. I yanked at his hair and shook him.

"Leave her alone," I growled.

He must not have seen it coming as he grovelled and winced in pain and let go of my daughter. I kept my hold on his hair until something hard, like a rock, struck my leg without my knowing. I staggered,

Then, another over my head, my vision became blurred

Then, two white dots appeared from a distance into the woods. It had to be touch lights, and through its rays, I noticed he was going for Klair again.

I reached for his leg, and I grabbed onto it as he jerked me off. I fastened my grip until my world turned dark, and then I prayed with my last breath that Klair would be okay.

Her name was beautiful, I birth it from my name.

The Blurred Line
(Book Three Except)
With her memory back, will she take back her life?

Chapter I

Ryan

It was June 11, 2021, and I rummaged through the pile of files, flipping through the pages as my eyes scanned the document, the numbers in it showing nonsense. Of course, the discrepancy was there. I only needed to look at the right place to see it. I had become an assistant art director at the museum not for loving arts but to track down a notorious art piece forger named Annette Khan, who has been terrorizing the art world. A criminal great at her craft. All the paper trails I could trace had led me to the Gevi Art Museum in Calitain. Therefore, I took the duty to go undercover. Obtaining the job as assistant director was almost effortless, as I already had experience in art from a previous operation. I never thought it would be helpful to someday. As I got the job, I took on the alias of Ryan Towson.

When I had the answer, I knew Khan had to be making profits from the forgery. Then again, it caught my attention since nothing appeared missing in accounting. The one in charge tried to keep the numbers and details untouched, a perfect accounting job.

The investigation lingered until a year in. Everyone in the museum was a suspect to me, especially Deby, the museum curator, so I got closer to her. I had observed her enough and had abundant experience at my job to know the right thing to say and do, so we clicked and began dating—my investigation into finding Annette Khan had not ceased during our time together.

After two months of dating Deby, she brought it up to me. She had noticed discrepancies in the accounting books and convincingly knew who it was. She took me by surprise. "How would she know if I don't, after all this time investigating Khan?"

I remember muttering to myself. Deby told me she would meet an informant who knew the inconsistency. I didn't mention Annette to her because the trail would eventually lead to her anyway, and just in case she missed a step and didn't figure it had to do with Annette, I didn't want to risk the investigation. Then, I agreed with Deby to meet the informant and let me know the conclusive evidence she received from the investigation.

It would seem almost unbelievable that the investigation rested without advances. I was stuck. On May 19, 2022, I sat and looked at the skewed numbers, clearly, con artist's work — my bet would probably be on Luke. I never trusted him — that is, the embezzlement of funds from the museum, but I have an inkling that there might be more to it than what meets the eye. But I'm unable to pinpoint it. I will pull another document from the filing cabinet when my phone rings.

I push my hand down into my pocket and fish out my phone. "Klair," I whisper to myself. I picked up the call, and there was no response on the other end, only static.

I furrow my brows. Getting a text message from Klair is not strange, but its content made me uneasy.

At Sonia's. Met her at the nursing home.

A minute goes by as I stare at her words before I realize. I realize that what I have been suspecting might be true. My eyes widen. If my theory was correct, then perhaps things would make sense. After Deby's accident, I found myself stuck in the same spot in the case for too long, and finally, I may have a breakthrough, a crack in the wall that might see me solving the case once and for all. All I have to do is to keep digging.

The first thing I have to confirm is an address. I checked Klair's address and compared it with the address Luke had invited his co-workers for a celebration, of some sort. And like I had suspected, they are different. As far as I know, Klair and Luke are still married, not separated or divorced. *So why on earth would they have different home addresses?* I think to myself. As I take the doubt in, something else catches my eye. I've seen the address Luke gave his co-workers before, but I'm unsure where.

I follow my instinct as I pull up Sonia's profile on my phone and scroll down until I find the address. The address matches the one Luke claims to have. *How is that possible? What on earth is going on? Is Sonia more than an employee to Luke, or is there some arrangement no one at the museum is aware of?* The multiple questions squirm in my head at the same time. As I wave them off, the one question I should focus on takes over my mind: Is her name truly Sonia?

I gather the files I had raked through for the past hour and put them back in the cabinet, except for a few that bear cogent and irrefutable evidence of the discrepancy in the museum's account. To some extent, the museum was stolen, and I wouldn't give the responsible a chance to get away with it, especially when it could lead me to napping Khan once and for all.

I fold the files and put them in the inside pocket of my jacket. Then, I exit the accounting department. When I return to my office, I take off my coat and hang it around my seat. I pull open one of my drawers, dip my hand under the pile of stacked papers, and fish out a burner phone I had stashed there. I switch it on and dial a number. It rings. I listen as it clicks.

"Hello, can you help me run a background check on Sonia Polinski? I want everything you have on her," I say into the phone.

"Hi, I'm fine, thank you for asking," says a voice at the other end of the line.

"I don't have time to exchange pleasantries, Rick. I need those details, please," I hear a sigh from him. "Now." I insist, sucking my teeth in irritation.

"Okay. It's all right, stranger. I'm on it as we speak," Rick replies as I hear his keyboard's sharp and rapid clicking sound in the background. I close my eyes and wait as patiently as I can muster.

I hold one hand, pressing the phone to my ear, while the other cups my forehead. I let my mind graze over the facts I have discovered and observed in this case. I think about the inconsistency in the museum's accounts, which affirmed my suspicion that someone was stealing from the museum. I think about the accident that condemned poor Deby to a hospital bed with life support strapped to her body for about eight months now. I think about the different addresses. Klair claims she has lost her memory, but that is yet to be established as a fact, so I don't know where that leads. Whenever I investigate a case, I feel like a hound sniffing around for a scent that will lead me to the truth. Knowing how to sniff for the truth is paramount in a world built on lies. And the moment my nose latches on a scent, I find it hard to stop. I'm unable to until I get to the truth.

"Well, it's been long since we've seen you around here, mate. Don't you think you've been out for too long? When are you coming back, Ryan?" Rick asks, interrupting my train of thought. I heave a sigh. It has been two years since I left the FBI to take this job. I have had ups and downs and sometimes miss being an FBI agent. I miss the life, the assorted cases to choose from, having a partner and a badge, the adrenaline that comes with tracking down dangerous, hardened criminals, and the instant respect whenever I announce that I am an FBI agent. I do miss nearly all of it, but now that I am finally onto something concrete in my case, I cannot afford to get distracted.

"Well, I can't leave in the middle of my case while it's unsolved, can I? Not especially when I am getting somewhere substantial right now.

The quicker you can get me all the information I need, the sooner I can solve this case," I say in a more demanding tone.

"Are you saying you are coming back after solving this case?" Rick asks. I can hear the excitement brewing in his voice. I can't help the grin that takes over my face.

"Yes, Rick. Yes. That's exactly what I'm saying," I reply, unwilling to let my voice's excitement disappear. "Now, please, do you have something for me?"

"Yes, of course. So, your Sonia Polinski doesn't exist."

"Mm?" I reply, standing up from my seat. I start pacing the room.

"Technically, yes. It's an alias."

"An alias? For who?"

"For a woman named Lily Bryan."

"Wait, I've heard that name before," I say, racking my brain to remember.

"Of course, you have. She's the queen of con artists. She's like a chameleon, changing her identity to whatever she wants, just like normal people changing their clothes daily. She is highly skilled and clever. She has managed to assimilate herself into different high social circles for her benefit while also evading every law enforcement agency in the country like a pro," Rick clarifies.

I clench my fist until I feel a little twinge in my knuckles. The realization that I've had her in front of me for all these months and been clueless about her motives disappoints me. And it also makes me wonder if Sonia knows who I am, that I am an FBI agent working undercover to capture criminals just like her.

"You almost sound like you admire her," I answer between gritted teeth.

"Of course, why wouldn't I? I admire anyone who is good at their job. That's why I admire you," he says, taking a breath given my silence. "I'll send you the recent pictures of Sonia we have on our database right away for visual confirmation," he adds.

My phone buzzes. I pick it up from my desk and tap on the new notification. I stare at the picture of Sonia or Lily dressed up as Klair. In the picture, she's walking out of Mary Oaks Nursing Home with Lair Cruz, Klair's mother. My phone buzzes again. It's another photo of Sonia dressed up as Klair, but this time, she's with Luke in the picture.

"Whoa," I yell, my eyes widening.

"Yes. According to these records, Sonia and Luke have been together for about two years now, even before Klair's accident, which supposedly claimed her memory. And from what we have seen so far, we have reasons to think Klair and Luke are Sonia's next targets," Rick says.

"But why? Why would she target a couple that's trying to run a museum? What is she hoping to gain? Money? Pieces of art? Power?" I ask aloud, rhetorically. My head feels like it's about to explode. I run my fingers through my hair and let out another sigh.

"Well, Lily Bryan is like a shark. The moment she smells blood in the water, she does not relent until she has taken a big chunk of a bite. She does a lot of work on shady business for politicians and super-rich people, Ryan. I mean, compelling and deep-pocketed people who are powerful enough to sink a whole city with the snap of their fingers."

I shake my head. "Not under my watch," I say under my breath. A few seconds of silence take over the call, and it suddenly occurs to me that Sonia had strategically inserted herself into Luke's life to be close to him. She had found a way to wriggle her way into his affairs to not only infiltrate Luke and Klair's marriage but also gain access to the museum and get her hands on sensitive materials she could use for her gain. But to what end? What is Sonia after? As Rick had implanted, it became pronounced that Sonia could not work alone. She must have had the backing of influential people to pull off these stunts while avoiding the FBI. Then again, who would these people be? What would they want? And how does this connect with discrepancies in the museum's accounts and Deby's accident? I realize I still have a lot to figure out, or my leads concerning this case would grow cold.

Then, something clicks in my consciousness. I recall something that could be important for the case. The canvas. The plain canvas and the name Kultant. And this could only lead to one thing.

"Sonia is working for the senate elect? What does Klair hold over him? The ledger which caused Deby's accident?" I ask on the phone.

"I don't know, Ryan," Rick replies. "I guess you need to talk to Sonia. Do you know where she is?"

"No, I don't. But I know exactly where Klair is."

"What?"

"Look, Rick, I have to go. Thanks for your help. I'll call you if I need anything else," I say, hanging up.

If Klair is one of Sonia's targets, she could be in danger now. I returned my burner phone to the drawer before picking up my phone, keys, and jacket. I rush down the stairs, bumping into people and muttering sorry. When I get to the parking lot, I push the button on my car key and hear a beeping sound.

As I pulled out of the parking lot, the tyres screeched against the tarmac, and I remembered Klair had sent me a text about an hour ago. So, I decided to call her. As I drift into the street, I hear the ringing.

"Please, pick up. Pick up," I say as I listen to the buzzing. It goes to voicemail.

"Jesus Christ!" I say under my breath. I call again. Voicemail. There is no point in leaving a voice message. If I don't get to that address in time, it'll be too late; I could feel it. I almost break all the traffic rules I know as I speed towards the address, finding it hard to keep cool.

Ten minutes later, I got to the address, panting and a bit sweaty. Perhaps I would have patted myself on the back for my excellent driving skills, but as I nosed into the driveway of the address, I first noticed a lot of blue and red lights. Several police cars line up the road on either side.

Klair, I think to myself. I look around to see if there's an ambulance. There's none. I switch off my car engine and get out of the car. I walk towards the house but stop short in my tracks.

Two police officers lead Klair out of the house by the arms. Her hands are cuffed. Completely unexpected. She bows her head as they lead her to one of the waiting police cars. Just as she's about to be shoved into the vehicle, she looks up and sees me looking at her. Our eyes are fixed on each other for a moment before a hand grabs her head and pushes her down into the vehicle, slamming the door behind her.

Chapter II

Klair

Outside the Calitain's police station, precinct 7 is quiet. With my arrest and Kultant's involvement, I thought there would be streams of reporters, but there are none. I tap my foot against its concrete floor as I wait for my ride.

Kultant had elicited my father's help to get the evidence from me. I scoff at the memory of him playing a fool in front of me. Trying to be a father, when we all know, Kultant must have had something on him for him to have made that trip.

I wonder what he told the officers, and how he explained away my relationship with him. It's questionable how many horrible people I am surrounded by.

A black car pulls up into the parking lot, as if on cue and I stare in disbelief. I only hope he isn't here for me.

Luke steps out of the car in a brown t-shirt with folded edges and worn-out blue jeans. His hair is dishevelled. I don't see the handsome put-together Luke I knew when I had the memory loss. He is just a regular person who I couldn't care less about.

His eyes scan the area. The neatly trim flower fence around the building does not pique his interest, as he slowly looks away. The concrete flooring beneath my feet feels uncomfortable as his footsteps approach me. His eyes catch mine. He increases his pace.

"Klair, you're out!" He exclaims, and I don't bother with a response. I fold my arms, tapping my foot against the floor, to a rhythm only I can hear.

"So, how did you even get out? You should be locked up"

A small tug to my lips remains. I know it's only been two hours since my arrest. I won't call that luck. I had expected a longer time in jail - life, perhaps.

Besides, his question does not seem like one that needs an answer. How did I get out? It seems rather rhetorical. We live in Calitain, a city where corruption is at its core. A question like that should not even be thought of, much less should it be asked.

If I can wire a few hundred dollars to the poor officers or link myself to the senator of Calitain, my deadbeat dad who finally visited me in jail, then staying there isn't an option.

I imagine him desperately trying to come up with something to describe our relationship, enough to convince them to release me.

Who did he tell them I was? A scholarship student? Poor individual of the state, who couldn't afford a lawyer or one whom the justice system had failed, except a senator like himself stepped in? I scoff at the pathetic excuses, but I can't be fazed. I don't care enough anymore.

"Are you listening to me?"

"Shut up, Luke! What do you want?" I snap, locking a glare on him. His expression changes quickly. His brows are raised, and his eyes don't hold much authority anymore. He rubs his palms on his jeans, and throws them up, backing up from me.

"F...fine," he stammers and walks a little further away.

"Since you so desperately want to know" I cross my two hands over my chest " My release was because of a testimony from a witness who appeared all of a sudden" I clap my hand, "to give a statement, saying that he knew my mum and she had died from heart attack, which perhaps," I place my hands over my waist "the witness didn't have any phone at that moment to call 191 for her treatment. How ridiculous, right?" I look up at Luke, with a burning gaze.

"Anyway," I continue, directing my stare toward the parking lot. "The same witness happened to know so much about me, yet all this while," I let out a dry laugh, leading to an uncomfortable cough. " when I had the memory loss, he didn't tell me that my mother's body was in the basement."

I am done playing the fool. Speaking of fools, he was one all along. Thinking he was playing me when he was the one being played.

He backs away

"Now, the reason why I'm here." He places his hand over his waist, trying to assert authority "What did you talk about with Sonia?" His voice is slightly raised. A small tug plays on my lips. It's funny that he is the same guy I used to think so highly of. He now looks skittish, like a little boy, who can't do anything without his mum.

"Are you listening to me?"

"Quiet down, Luke. You are way too loud. I'm just trying to enjoy my peace, out here." Luke flinches, which is completely alien to me.

"Are you kidding me?" His voice is in a low pitch.

"Now, that's the tone I'm looking for," I monotone. "Do you know that Sonia was a part of Dablo?"

His forehead creases in confusion, and I can't tell if he's being honest. "What the hell is that?"

I revel in satisfaction as the cluelessness plays on his face. A smug smile lingers on my lips. I'm finally one step ahead of him. "You tell me,"

He presses his thumb and index finger to his forehead as he paces. I roll my eyes at his pathetic response.

It crosses my mind that, he may know, and he is trying to play on my intelligence, but I shrug it off. I am tired of being on the clueless end.

I watch as a grey truck pulls into the police station's lot. I wave at the dark-haired gentleman as he steps out and walks towards me. "Thank you, Ryan, for picking me up." He straightens out his shirt, smiles, and nods at me.

"Hey! Where are you going?" Luke calls after me "Where are you taking her?" He gestures to Ryan. "Watch where you are going, you dimwit, she is still my wife, you know?" he says, his hands placed on his waist as I throw him a glance.

"Were we married Luke?" I say with exasperation - my hand covering my mouth, as a gasp escapes my lips in feigned surprise. "Then I should be home before dinner to make you your favorite meal." I wear the most convincing expression of honesty as I look into his eyes. Everything about him throws me off, and I am mostly disgusted by the level of audacity he possesses.

He coaxes his head, "You know?"

"Of course, I do, Luke. I remember everything. Did you think I would forget?" I walk slowly towards him, "Did you, husband?"

"I remember how you hit me in the head with a rock, you fool." I jab my finger through his chest with all the strength I can gather, earning me a painful groan from him. "I remember you killed my mum because she tried to stop you from running after me. You were going to pin her murder on me"

"Are you sure Klair?" his lips curl into a frown.

I scoff at his gaslighting, which used to work on me "Luke. I remember that you never even regarded me as anything. Oh, don't get me started on how much I remember. I remember how I began to hate you, Luke. And no, sweetheart, I don't hate you any less."

I feel an arm rest on my shoulder, and I look over to see Ryan standing there with concern etched into his features.

"Klair," he starts, and I exhale, returning my attention to Luke. He stares at me, as if waiting for a change of heart. He looks stupid.

"Now, mummy's boy," I pause, scanning his face for any trace of fear I can find. I revel in that for a while. He looks offended by my choice of words, but his silence shows that he can do nothing about it. I am not afraid of him any more.

"Run to mummy, like you always do." I turn toward Ryan as I walk toward the car

Ryan walks over to his car, just a few feet from us, he holds the door open for me, as I walk towards it, climbing in. I watch Luke walk away.

"I don't know if this is the right time to tell you this," Ryan says, as he keys in the ignition.

"What is it?"

"Someone broke into my office today."

"What?"

"Yeah"

"Oh, no.. did they steal anything?"

"The canvases Klair," He says lowering his eyes to the car's dashboard "They are gone."

"Let them have it, they can't use it anyway."

Don't miss out!

Visit the website below and you can sign up to receive emails whenever Zee David publishes a new book. There's no charge and no obligation.

https://books2read.com/r/B-A-VIWU-INMBC

BOOKS 2 READ

Connecting independent readers to independent writers.

Did you love *The Unfinished Line*? Then you should read *The Blurred Line*[1] by Zee David!

With her memory back
 The line, now blurred; begging the question
 Who is Klair running from- someone or herself?
 Read Klair Knox's mystery as the suspense continues: Book Three

---

1. https://books2read.com/u/bMn9a8

2. https://books2read.com/u/bMn9a8

About the Author

Zee David is a nurse by profession but sees writing as a passion. She discovered the talent at an early age. To her, the greatest gift. Her satisfaction is knowing that her work is read and loved.

She loves writing, watching Korean dramas, and most of all, she loves her family.

Zee David's language background is reflected in her work, which consists of French, American, and British English. She speaks four languages fluently.

She is an animal lover, especially cats, and dogs.

Reads a lot, though mostly listens to audiobooks. She doesn't have a favourite author, though leans toward the mystery genre.

Zee also writes, other genres though under another pen name.